The Footprints And Other Stories

A collection of science fiction short stories including; Humour; Post-apocalyptic; Space Adventures; Mysteries; Paranormal; Time Travel; & Robots.

By Brian Terence

Dedication.

To my wife for all her love and patience.

Contents

Dedication. ii
Reviews & Connect. vii
THE OLDEST FOOTPRINTS 1
   Authors Notes: 2
   Introduction. 3
   Chapter 1. 6
   Chapter 2. 10
   Chapter 3. 13
   Chapter 4. 20
   Chapter 5. 21
   Chapter 6. 29
   Chapter 7. 33
   Chapter 8. 45
   Chapter 9. 51
   Chapter 10. 71
   Chapter 11. 74
   Chapter 12. 77
   Chapter 13. 83
   Chapter 14. 85
   Chapter 15. 88
   Chapter 16. 93
   Chapter 17. 96
   Chapter 18. 97
   Chapter 19. 101
   Chapter 20. 103
   Chapter 21. 109
   Chapter 22. 112

Chapter 23. 121
Chapter 24. 128
Chapter 25. 134
Chapter 26. 136
Chapter 27. 140
Chapter 28. 142
'To Have And To Hold' 143
Authors Notes:..144
Chapter 1. 145
Chapter 2. 153
Chapter 3. 158
Terminal Vision 163
Authors Notes:..164
Chapter 1. 165
Chapter 2. 170
Chapter 3. 176
Chapter 4. 182
Chapter 5. 185
Chapter 6. 195
Chapter 7. 199
Chapter 8. 201
Ahead In Time 203
Authors Notes:..204
Chapter 1. 205
Chapter 2. 211
Chapter 3. 214
Chapter 4. 217
An Archaeological Twist..........................223

Authors Notes: 224
Chapter 1. 225
Chapter 2. 227
Chapter 3 230
Beneath The City Of The Ancients 231
Authors Notes: 232
Chapter 1. 233
Chapter 2. 239
Chapter 3. 244
The Words Of The Sole 251
Authors Notes: 252
I'm An Angel, Not An Astrophysicist! 259
Authors Notes: 260
'Never Mess With The Cleaner ' 273
Authors Notes: 274
Chapter 1 – Anubis? 275
Chapter 2 – 'Henry' Uses His Head 279
Chapter 3 – What's The Plural Of Anubis? 282
Chapter 4 – It's Not A Mask. 284
Chapter 5 - Sorry I don't speak Dog. 286
About the Author. 291
Acknowledgements. 293

Copyright – Brian Terence 2024

I assert the moral right to be identified as the author of this work.

"No part of this book may be used or reproduced in any manner for the purpose of training artificial intelligence technologies or systems"

Reviews & Connect.

If you enjoy this story, please leave a review/follow me on either Amazon or Goodreads:

https://www.amazon.com/author/brianterence

https://www.goodreads.com/author/show/52410012.Brian_Terence

Connect with me on BlueSky or LinkedIn :

uk.linkedin.com/in/brianterence42

@brianterence.bsky.social

THE OLDEST FOOTPRINTS ...

"You will know the truth, and the truth will set you free." – John 8:32

How the truth of humanity's origins would free a nation from tyranny. How the search for that truth would free a heartbroken widower from the pain of grief.

Authors Notes:

The idea for this story came from listening to an astronomy podcast; they were discussing the planet Jupiter. During the program, one of the experts mentioned that the moon Callisto had the oldest surface in the solar system. This started me thinking that if there were a single place that might have evidence of an alien visit to our system, it would be on Callisto.

This story is the result of that original idea, as with many stories, it has taken on a life of its own; there are several versions available.

It is my intention to write a version with several endings and allow the reader to choose which they prefer.

The Oldest Footprints ...

Introduction.

Julian Richards carefully brushed away the layers of dust and grit and wiped a tear from his eye. Whether the dust of the Gobi desert was irritating his eye or he was crying wasn't clear. He worked methodically to reveal the intricate details of the ancient footprint. It seemed to tell a story of a creature that had roamed these lands millions of years ago. Yet, the imprint appeared so fresh and well-preserved, almost as if the dinosaur had just strolled across the hill moments ago. Out of the corner of his eye, he saw his wife working away next to him, but when he turned, of course, she was gone. It was just his imagination playing a cruel trick on him, again. As Julian continued to brush away the dust and grit that obscured the remarkable find, he gripped his brush tightly as though he could hold his emotions in check by physical effort.

He raised himself up and heard his back crack. Looking out over the landscape, it reminded him of his home in Alberta, Canada. It was the fantastic discoveries, not far from his childhood home, that had given him his interest, some might say obsession, in fossils.

His discovery of these fossilised footprints reminded him of a bittersweet memory from his last trip to the beach with his beloved wife. They had walked along the shore, watching their footprints vanish with each gentle wave, prompting his wife to reflect on the fleeting nature of human life. The pain hit him like a punch, the emotion causing an actual physical reaction. A woman of barely fifty should never have died so young, but even in the twenty-second century, there were some conditions that couldn't be fixed.

She contrasted their footprints with Julian's work, delving into the ancient footprints of dinosaurs and early humans, some fossilised for millions of years. Even the astronauts' footprints on the moon might endure for aeons, while hers were vanishing as quickly as she made them. In that poignant moment, she encouraged Julian to cherish their happy memories, but to also embrace the present and future. She urged him to continue leaving his own footprints on the world, just as he had been doing through his groundbreaking research —

"Dr Richards, Julian, there's a call for you." His assistant shouted.

"Okay, I'm on my way. Who is it? Did they say what they wanted?" he asked.

"It was the university switchboard. Not sure who is asking for you?"

Julian took the phone, "Yes, it's Dr Richards. How can I help? May I ask whom I'm talking to, please?" He stood listening, his jaw hanging open. His disbelief was total.

After hanging up the call, he stood there staring at the phone in amazement. Unable to contain his curiosity, his assistant asked, "So, who was it, Dr Richards?"

Dr Julian Richards's reply was distant and distracted. "It was NASA!"

Chapter 1.

The reflected Texas sunlight was shining right in Isaiah's eyes, and he repositioned. The chair squeaked, and several people glared at him as though his movements had implied boredom. Really, anyone who wasn't bored by this meeting was already brain-dead. This was the embodiment of the 'this-meeting-should-have-been-an-email' meme. For most of his friends, working for NASA was a glamorous and exciting job. Sure, but not the bits involving HR, budgets, and a report from the guy who counted paper clips!

He risked another glance out of the window. He could see the coffee stand. Maybe someone had turned down the aircon, got to save the planet, or what's left of it after the sea surges. The room felt hot and stuffy, and he was half-asleep. The complex was barely thirty years old, but nothing quite worked right. Funds had been tight at the time, a major war would do that. And then the sudden sea surge forced the move out of Florida before they all got their feet wet.

He needed a coffee. The lady who ran the small stall made homemade pastries to go with the coffee. He could almost taste the crumbly, warm texture. The smell of the fresh coffee. His mouth was watering at the thought ...

There was a loud scraping noise as the woman next to him got out of her chair. She looked at him oddly. Had he dosed off? He started to grab his things and get up. Finally, he could get that coffee...

"Isaiah, Charity, can you wait a moment? I need a word." The Director said it in a normal, almost bored tone. But despite this, Isaiah felt sweat break out on his forehead. He and Charity from HR, what had he done? Was he going to get a dressing down for dosing off during the meeting?

There was an ominous pause. Several people, including the woman he'd been sitting next to, looked on with approval. Frank, being a wind-up as always, made a throat-slitting gesture and grinned as he walked out the door.

All thoughts of coffee and fresh pastries disappeared from his mind as his eyes followed Frank out the door. He glimpsed two large men in suits, a frightened-looking kid wedged between them and another suited guy who looked 'Security' for no specific reason you could identify.

Once the newcomers were all inside, one of the large men in the suits locked the door. Isaiah didn't even know the door could be locked.

"Isaiah, Charity, this meeting is not taking place, and anything discussed in this room must not go any further until an official position has been agreed. Am I clear?" The 'Suit' stated firmly.

Isaiah looked at his boss for confirmation. he nodded once, so Isaiah confirmed that he'd comply. But Charity was made of stronger stuff and turned on the 'Suit', demanding to know who the f'ing hell he thinks he is. Isaiah was sure the language she was using violated every rule in the HR manual, the one that she had written.

The Director spoke to Charity in a reassuring tone, but Isaiah could pick up a note of desperation in his voice. Whatever had the boss disturbed would be worth hearing. "Please, Charity, I assure you that you are going to want to hear this and that your input will be invaluable." A little pacified, Charity nodded her acquiescence.

The Suit looked relieved. Isaiah thought he might actually be scared of Charity, which proved that he wasn't stupid. Anyone who wasn't at least a little nervous, either didn't know her or was too stupid to be scared.

"I'm with the NASA Security Team. My identity isn't important. We have a situation and need your input on a very sensitive matter, hence the need for secrecy." He gestured for the young lad to come forward, asking him to present a report.

The lad looked anxious, but he obviously knew what he was doing. The large main screen lit up with a view of what was clearly the Jupiter system. These must have been images from the latest Jupiter mission, 'Juno Seven'. The data from the fly-bys of the moons had been coming in for days, which explained the kid's presence. He was possibly an analyst. What had they found that required this level of secrecy?

Chapter 2.

Each of Jupiter's four Galilean moons was unique. The image they were looking at was obviously Callisto, photos of the surface both at a distance of a few hundred kilometres and then closer as the craft entered an elliptical orbit, swinging out and then back in close for a low-altitude pass. The surface was covered in craters. The contrast between the white and the dark areas was stark in the photos, almost exaggerated.

Another series of images followed, including a close-up of a crater, the bottom covered in dust that might not have been disturbed in four billion years. The image was adjusted, and a line swept the picture as it was again zoomed in and digitally cleaned. A set of footprints was clearly visible across the crater. They could have been from the Moon. There wasn't anything unusual about them.

Then Isaiah Wilson sat bolt upright in his chair and asked that the previous image be shown again. The 'Suit' gestured to the technician, a slight smile touching the corners of his mouth but not his eyes.

"This image is Callisto? There's no chance this image could be of the Moon?" Isaiah asked, his voice tight.

Charity was puzzled, "What's odd about the footprints? They look like countless images I've seen taken from the Moon and some from Mars, although the colours are wrong for Mars. What am I missing?"

The question hung in the air for a few moments, the Director unwilling to give away the answer, wanting them to work it out.

"No one has set foot on Callisto yet. The Moon and Mars have had people on them for decades. But the trip to Callisto is five to seven years. No one has walked on it. No human being, that is. Callisto has the oldest surface in the solar system. Those footprints could be millions of years old." Isaiah's tone conveyed the awe he was feeling.

"Billions, even." Added the NASA Director. "The surface of Callisto is billions of years old. With no atmosphere to erode the footprints and no volcanism to cover them, they could be nearly as old as the solar system, roughly four billion years."

"This is the maximum resolution obtainable from the camera. There isn't enough detail to estimate the age by counting the micrometeor impacts within the footprints. But if they are millions or billions of years old .... " The Director left the comment hanging in the air.

Charity asked the question that was on everyone's mind, "Who the bloody hell left those footprints then?"

Chapter 3.

The NASA Director looked at Charity and said, "The reason for this meeting is to get your initial thoughts as to what, if anything, we should do about the Footprints? Do you feel a mission is important? Do we have anyone who could handle a five to seven-year mission?" Turning to Isaiah, he said, "Is it mechanically possible? There are the new sleeper units, but have they been adequately tested?"

Isaiah hesitated for some time, thinking about his responses before saying anything. Charity was also evidently considering her words.

Finally, Isaiah felt he had to break the silence. "Who knows about this find? Anyone outside of this room? What impact will this have on our relationship with the US "government", with Richmond?'" The word government was in speech marks. How legitimate it was, and how fair the recent elections were, was very much an open question. Was winning a fifth term really confirmation of 'God's blessing'? These were questions no one dared to ask unless you really wanted to disappear in the middle of the night, never to be seen again.

"No one knows anything outside of this room. This technician had the sense to bring these finds to me discretely as soon as it was clear what they were. Once I'd ruled out the possibility of a practical joke, I needed to bring more people in on this. Hence, this little get-together. The gents in the suits are our internal security team. I've asked them not to give their names for their own protection." The Director kind of ran down. He'd brought Charity and Isaiah in on this without asking them first. It could be their death sentence.

"Yeah, most of the 'America Reborn' mob don't even believe in dinosaurs. Aliens would completely smash their whole worldview." Charity said cynically.

Isaiah thought Charity has had more reason than most to be cynical. The only good thing about 'America Reborn', was they weren't racists. And that was the only good thing. So, the colour of Charity's skin wasn't an issue, but the fact that she had ovaries was a real problem. Hyper-chauvinistic was too small a word for their attitude toward women.

Isaiah said after a short pause. "Well, the footprints have been there for anything up to four billion years. Would another decade or two make any difference? I'd surely love to find out who left those footprints. But if they were left by Martian explorers, for example, we know they must be long gone. We've not found so much as a rusty nail on Mars to show that anyone lived there. So that either means they lived so long ago that nothing could remain, or they never existed in the first place. It would be ironic if we learned of the existence of ancient Martians from their footprints left on Callisto rather than Mars itself. But then Mars is much more active, so it's probable that any trace of them was wiped away. If those are artificial rather than some weird trick of the light, I would guess they'd be from a civilisation indigenous to this system. Given that both Earth and Mars were inhabitable for billions of years, It's more likely that they came from either of those worlds than from another star, but I'd be lying if I said I didn't want to find out. Regardless, it will be an Earth-shaking discovery. But all that said, if we go in ten years or fifty years, will it really change anything? They'll still be there. Maybe waiting until the current political difficulties blow over?"

Charity asked, "You mentioned Earth and Mars. Are you thinking they could be footprints from an ancient Earth civilisation?"

"You mean, am I suggesting that ancient Atlanteans travelled to Callisto and went for a stroll? Obviously, no, but given how active the Earth's surface is, we might never know if there was a human or other type of civilisation that existed hundreds of thousands to millions of years ago. Nothing would have survived. Again, Callisto's unique surface is a time capsule. We might find out about our own past by going to Jupiter." Isaiah said.

The Director then dropped something of a bombshell, although it should have occurred to all of them. "What if they're not billions of years old? What about the possibility that the people that left them are still on Callisto? I mean, right now?"

The NASA director looked at Isaiah as if hoping for some counter comment, but Isaiah could only stare, his jaw hanging as he was lost in thought.

Alien visitors could be on the surface of Callisto right now!

"It's a very long trip. We'd have to adapt a Martian liner. They can carry over fifty for the journey to Mars, but this would be a much longer run. The ships rotate for gravity, but there's the radiation to consider. I could scan through our records, but there are not going to be many who would volunteer for this mission. It's a long time away from family. Given the duration, risks, and radiation, it could easily be a one-way trip for some. Even given the knowledge that they'd be going to investigate possible alien footprints, the duration would deter many." Charity was almost thinking aloud rather than explaining to the meeting.

"At least budget isn't a problem anymore. Even a couple of decades ago, we'd have never gotten this past the appropriations people. But now, with all the metals from the asteroids. We are richer than god, as they used to say." Isaiah grinned at his own lack of caution. Outside of the pseudo-diplomatic sanctity of NASA, he'd have been fined or even imprisoned for that remark.

The Suit then made another comment that significantly increased the complexity of preparing this mission, "Secrecy is paramount. Clearly, the mission to Jupiter will have to be made public, but its real reason must remain a secret. If it gets out that there might be little, or rather tall, green men wandering over Callisto's surface, there could be panic. Not to mention the reaction of the US administration."

"Why do you say tall?" asked Isaiah.

"The spacing between the footsteps suggests they were over two meters. Not impossible for a human, but they'd have to be tall." Was the Suits reply.

That left the room stunned, each assessing this revelation about the probable height of the visitors to Callisto.

Charity then said, "Forgive me, but just to check. Is there any possibility they could be native to Callisto? The lower gravity might explain their height."

"If it were Europa or Ganymede, I'd say it would be possible, but unless we've really got the details of the Solar System's formation wrong, there's no real chance they are indigenous. But your thought about lower gravity might imply that the Mars theory is more likely." The Director said.

Charity continued, "We'll, or rather, I'll have to review the records of every person worldwide?" The last was aimed at the Suit, who nodded. "That's got astronaut training and has domestic circumstances where a seven-year, possible one-way mission might be attractive. If I was still with my Ex, I might have volunteered myself. If it's going to be such a long mission, we might be better off with an all-female crew?" Again, she glanced around the room as if inviting feedback, but this was her speciality, so the responses were somewhat vague. "If women, then past childbearing age, because of the radiation. It better not be any men at all in case anyone gets pregnant en-route. And where the hell am I going to find a palaeontologist who's going to want to go to Jupiter?"

Isaiah reflected on her words about still being with her Ex, with the new 'Family Protection' laws. If Charity were still married, she wouldn't be allowed to work at all, far less go on a mission to Jupiter. How many women had been forced to make terrible sacrifices for their careers?

The Suit interrupted. "We may need to impose one person on the mission, a security officer, in the event the aliens are hostile. I've just the person in mind; his nickname is 'Dollars'. Isaiah, I believe you know him? He'll be listed as an 'extreme environment survival instructor.' He'll do that job, but if we're sending a ship to Jupiter to encounter possible aliens. Someone needs to have some military training."

"That's a big if," Said Isaiah, "If they're still there. If they're not long extinct. If they're not a trick of the light. Etc.

Chapter 4.

Dr Julian Richards's reply was distant and distracted. "It was NASA! They want to discuss the possibility of me going on a space mission."

"Where, to Mars? Maybe they've found fossils? That would be an incredible discovery. if you were associated with it, it would do wonders for your career." The assistant had images of awards and prestige dancing in his head. It might not hurt his own prospects, either.

"No, I don't think it was Mars. They said it could be a long-duration flight. My old military pilot training was one reason why they approached me. It's my expertise in rock structure they want, apparently. Not for fossils. Although it would be amazing to find a fossilised T-Rex footprint on the slopes of Olympus Mons."

"So, what now? Do we have time to finish up here, or should I begin packing up the equipment?" The assistant asked.

"No, there's no rush. They'll not be leaving next week. The arrangement is that I'll meet them at the end of the month. But I confess I'm too distracted to concentrate today. Let's finish and find something to eat." Dr Julian concluded.

Chapter 5.

"Dr Julian Richards, welcome to NASA. I trust your journey was okay?" The receptionist asked blandly, polite yet emotionless.

Of course, thought Julian, it's a Robot. NASA could afford them. It had a vaguely female face, and it was androgynous but definitely not male. He confirmed he'd survived the flight and chauffeured drive. That had been a human. Looking around, there was no one in sight. He felt oddly alone with the robot.

"Let me take you through to the meeting room. Many of the others are already here. Most of the astronauts are based locally. You are one of the last to arrive." The receptionist led him through multiple sets of security doors and along corridors. Without the robot's guidance, he'd never find his way out.

The robot knocked curtly on the door, although why he felt a robot could exhibit such an emotion. He wasn't sure, nor why he thought the robot was irritated with him for making it direct him. Anthropomorphism, clearly. He never understood women. Dinosaurs, rock, and anything else long dead was an open book. But women, no chance. The thought of death reminded him of the one woman he had come close to understanding, but she was now gone.

The robot opened the door and closed it behind him. Out of habit, he smiled at her and said thank you. But she turned abruptly and walked off. He felt almost hurt by her rapid departure, the sense that he'd offended her still haunting him.

"... Yes, John, there were two casualties in the attack. Two unidentified children's bodies were discovered in the ruins of the building. The Senate has condemned the attack. A group, self-styled 'Feminist Action', claims responsibility for the attack. Although they, of course, claim the building was empty at the time of the explosion. Long Live the Patriarch." The TV news report finishing with the usual salute to the 'Father of the Nation'.

As he entered the room, there was a surprise in store: It wasn't a meeting room as he'd expected it to be. It was more of a lounge, with chairs and small tables scattered about. The other surprise was that he was the only man in the room unless they were all hiding in the gents. Several dozen people were milling about, chatting and eating nibbles. Everyone was female, all of different races, but of uniform height and build. He knew the last was practicality for space suits, etc. Not relating to fashion, the enlightened twenty-second century didn't worry about stereotypes of female beauty. He heard his wife's voice in his head say – 'Yeah, right' (with her ironic eye role). The other thing of note was that most were at least his age. Almost none appeared below fifty. This wasn't that odd for astronauts, but was there a specific reason why no one was younger?

He could overhear several conversations expressing disbelief at the news report. One woman said, "Why would there be two kids in an otherwise empty government office building at three AM? Do they think anyone buys that crap?" Another finally turned off the TV in evident disgust.

He was standing somewhat uncertainly when he heard someone say, "Don't worry about that droid. She's programmed to be a bit odd with men. it was found that some men developed a bit of a crush on her if she was too feminine or friendly." The woman speaking was tall and powerfully built, with a mischievous grin. "Hi, I'm Charity, HR. Good to meet you, Dr Julian Richards."

Turning to the room, she introduced Julian. Then she said, "Okay, if I can get your attention, let's address the 'elephant in the room. '"

"You mean, why are we all old or all female? Which 'elephant' are you referring to?" Was one wisecrack from a woman in the centre of the small semicircle that had assembled at Charity's request.

"Good observation. Yes, there are two points to note. please listen first and then jump down my throat later, okay?" Charity looked frustrated. Most of the astronauts were international. Only she and the Captain were Americans, and the general resentment towards their government spilt over in the women's attitude to them.

"You're all past childbearing age, either naturally or because of medical complications, that's essential. The trip to Jupiter is a long one, so the radiation dosage will be higher than normal. You would have been strongly advised against having kids after this mission." There was a sharp intake of breath from many, but out of respect for Charity's words, they didn't interrupt. It was unclear whether it was the destination or radiation that caused the reaction.

"That is why you're all older; kids are no longer at the table for any of you. Assuming we've done our homework. If that is not the case, see me straight away, after this meeting, in private. The other reason should be obvious: female crews are more stable on long missions. We anticipate a crew of eleven, nine female, and two male. With three droids."

"Lucky men!" someone said.

"What's lucky, that they'll be stuck in a tin can with nearly a dozen menopausal women or that they're going to Jupiter?" Said another comedian.

The Captain, who, as the only American astronaut in the room, had been shunned by everyone else, spoke up, stepping immediately into her role, and asked, "So why any men at all? Wouldn't an all-female crew be best? Can't you find a female geologist? No disrespect to Dr Richards, but there are female geologists."

Charity felt a tightness in her throat. She couldn't even hint at the real reason why they needed the world-renowned expert on fossil footprints. For security reasons, they'd all agreed that not until the mission was on its way would the truth behind the mission and the urgency be explained to the crew.

"Dr Julian Richards is an expert in his field. Another is time. We have a small window when the three planets are in the optimum position. It will be some years before the Earth, Mars, and Jupiter are in such a fuel-efficient alignment. The two males will be Dr Richards and a military survival trainer. The reason for them is simple: although there are females with equal competence, they are all younger, have kids, or are in long-term relationships, which would disqualify them immediately. Dr Richards also has some military pilot training, including orbital craft. That will reduce the training needed and give us an additional pilot if an emergency arises." Charity wanted to get this meeting back on track. They had a lot of ground to cover.

"So, we're all barren old spinsters, and that makes us disposable. So much for the enlightened twenty-second century! LONG LIVE THE PATRIARCHY!" The woman who had just spoken hadn't commented previously, but her words dripped with sarcasm as she imitated the sign-off of the TV news reporter. Julian couldn't identify her rank or speciality. Although her feelings were understandable, Julian thought her words were unfair. The NASA people were making every effort to plan a complicated space mission with a very tight range of crew parameters. The accusation seemed unfair to him, but then he wasn't a 'barren old spinster,' so how could he judge? He was just a heartbroken widower. If he was the best they could find, they must be desperate. Although it was better now, in the weeks after his wife's death, there had been days when Julian had forgotten to eat. Putting him on a spacecraft with many others depending on him was a scary responsibility.

The comments had caused a ripple to pass through the group, some supportive, others derisive.

Charity coughed quietly, and the room returned to a respectful silence. "The mission is expected to take five to seven years, depending on whether we slingshot past Mars. The OP team is calculating the options; there's not much time. We have got a launch window in a few months. Earth, Mars, and Jupiter are all moving into a good position for the trip, but soon, the Earth and Jupiter will be too far around the Sun from each other for a direct flight to be an option. The duration of the flight is another reason you've been selected. None of you are in long-term relationships or have dependants. Again, if that's wrong, please see me immediately. To summarise. Most of you are female, past childbearing age, shortish, and have no long-term relationships or dependents. We've gone through your files and shortlisted everyone in this room. Obviously, not all of you will want or be able to go."

"I'm not going to mince my words, ladies, gentleman – There's a real possibility that this will be a one-way trip. The risks are calculated to be slightly higher than the original Mars landing. You are going to be a long way from home, and a lot can go wrong." Charity's concluding comments left a sombre atmosphere in the room.

Chapter 6.

After Charity had finished her presentation, the meeting broke up, and everyone spread out into small groups, talking and enjoying the hospitality. Given the content of the presentation, none of the women wanted to speak with her, so she made her way straight towards Julian.

"I hope the comments didn't make you feel uncomfortable? You're one of the few non-astronauts on this mission." Charity said.

"Actually, I kind of share their confusion. I'm still not sure why I'm going either. Why would you need me on this trip? I can't say I'm not nervous. My longest tour of duty was only three months on a lunar patrol craft. Seven years is a very different level of commitment. As to why you need an expert on fossils on this mission remains unclear. Yes, I know it's my geological skills, being single, having no kids, and all that. But frankly, I don't believe you." Julian paused as he saw the concerned look in Charity's eyes. "My personal guess is that you've found footprints of little green men. Am I right?" He then winked conspiratorially. He decided to turn it into a joke. Perhaps the reaction of the others had unsettled her, but Charity wasn't happy.

"Yes, 'little green men,' you've discovered our secret. I know things must still be very raw for you. I know it's not been long since your wife's passing. I'm glad you made it here. I'm sure your insights will be invaluable. Stick with it if you can. My door is always open if you need to talk." With these parting words, Charity headed off towards a large group. Julian watched her as she walked away. Her reaction at the mention of the 'real reason' for him being included on this mission, was nearly as big a mystery as everything else about this assignment. So, his wife's death had opened this door for him. Well, there's always a silver lining. Did Charity and the others know how dysfunctional he was? The grief was crippling.

As he looked around the room, he heard his wife's voice in his head, 'Lucky you, stuck with all these beautiful women for years. With nothing else to do'. He almost felt her mischievously elbow him in the ribs.

He tried not to let his shattered heart show on his face, but he failed utterly. Fortunately, no one was paying him even the slightest attention.

After some time, in which Julian had managed to consume an improbable quantity of small somethings or others. The

Captain moved in his direction; she was the leader of the mission, and that made her his boss. Brushing the crumbs from his face, he held out his hand. She stared at him, clear hostility on her face. Whether it was his gender or his mere existence that irritated her remained unclear.

"Dr Julian Richards, I've read one of your books. Your analysis of dinosaur gait from fossil footprints was a first-class piece of work." Her words were polite enough, but there was a clear subtext. Why the hell is there an expert on fossils on MY mission? The word 'MY' was all caps. This was very much her expedition; the taxpayer's funding, NASA's planning, and the various techs that made it possible were irrelevant. Julian imagined that if she wanted to, she could make the ship fly by sheer force of will. He looked into her eyes, and they stared at each other for some time. The whole room seemed to pause. To Julian, the room fell silent, and there was no one else there.

They were the only people in the entire universe.

Maybe it was the intensity of his emotions, all that pent-up stress. The whole weird business with this meeting, even the apparent hostility that all the women were showing him. But to Julian's embarrassment, he felt strongly attracted to the Captain. It had been a long time since he'd been intimate with a woman. He hadn't even felt desire. Perhaps it was the imagined words of his wife a few moments earlier, but Julian Richards suddenly remembered that the world was full of beautiful women. It was such an unexpected inrush of feelings that he felt a little dizzy.

What the Captain thought about his strange facial expression wasn't clear. Dr Julian Richards excused himself and headed for the 'Gents' to splash cold water on his face.

Chapter 7.

Strangely, once the training actually began, his relationship with the other potential crew improved. They were all too busy to be hostile. All except the Captain, of course. She was still as aloof and distant as the Jovian system and nearly as deadly.

There was an additional complication. He was almost guaranteed a place. Everyone else, excluding the Captain, had to earn their seat, and this created more resentment.

On the third day of training, the Military Survival Instructor, the only other man on the mission, arrived. He saluted the Captain, and she returned the compliment, but it was clear she was no happier with him than she was with Julian. After Charity had done the general introductions, he wandered over to Julian and introduced himself in person.

"Hi, Dr Richards, it's great to meet you. I'm John Williams. – Like the composer. But everyone calls me 'Dollars' in reference to the prosthetic legs. They are supposed to be worth a billion dollars. The 'Brass' have made it clear that although I'm disposable on the mission, the legs aren't."

He shook Julian's hand and pulled his trouser leg up just enough to reveal the metallic prosthetic.

"Great in low gravity environments, but bugger all use for ballroom dancing!" Dollars grinned. "I understand that you've had some military pilot training yourself."

Julian knew this was just polite chat. The Officer had obviously read reports on all of the potential crew. However, Julian was surprised that he liked this opportunity to discuss slightly more recent history than the Cretaceous. "I was a pilot of a Lunar Patrol Runner, but they are tugboats compared to the beauty we'll be using for this journey. It's still hard to get my head around. I was in the Gobi a few weeks ago looking for dinosaur fossils, and now I'm here. Possibly going to Jupiter, it's a steep learning curve. I'm assuming we'll be getting in some time in orbit once all the medical and other pre-checks are completed?"

Dollars nodded confirmation, "It's great you're keen, Doc. The Captain and first officer will be handling most of the regular navigation. But we're the backup team. I promise we'll have plenty of opportunities to practice those high-G manoeuvres that were so common back in your day. We need you to be ready to handle an emergency if the main crew is incapacitated. Your presence on this mission may well be crucial, Dr Richards."

Julian got the distinct impression that there was more behind Dollar's last words than merely reassuring an old pilot that he'd get in some flying and wasn't an emergency spare only. What was really behind this mission?

..

The following weeks on the lunar training base became a blur. His enthusiasm for fossils had been something he'd shared with his wife. They were a team, working in the Gobi. Every new find was a reminder of her absence. But here, it was all new. His previous time in space had been long before they'd met, and so now, when something noteworthy happened, it didn't feel odd that he couldn't share it with her. He had a good relationship with 'Dollars'. Being the only two men meant that he thought they had to stick together. Given all that Dollars had been through, after all, you didn't get prosthetic legs out of choice. He wasn't bitter or resentful. Julian found himself becoming fond of Dollars and even started to enjoy his ribald comments.

There was considerable competition for the other spaces on the mission.

Competition that bordered on aggression at times, which surprised him. It was an opportunity of a lifetime. You'd be in the history books—the first crewed mission to Jupiter. However, the level of backbiting and aggression shown by many of the potential crew members was scary. Gossip and metaphorical stabs in the back. Despite her almost guaranteed place on the mission, the Captain received a lot of hostility. It had been let slip that the Captain was not part of the vetting team. After that, the claws were out. Her position as the only American on the mission added to her isolation. Many of the others holding her personally responsible for the sins of her government.

...

Dollars looked at the technician; there was a faint beading of sweat on his forehead. The atmosphere was carefully controlled. There was no reason for him to look so sweaty and dishevelled unless he had been running. But from where? Or he had a guilty conscience – But why thought Dollars? They helped people into their suits dozens of times a day. It was automatic muscle memory. But this guy was thinking about what he was doing. He was too old to be a trainee, not the new kid. From the look in his eyes, he'd been around. The guy was just all wrong, and Dollars didn't like the feel, the way he furtively glanced at Dollars, but tried to avoid looking at the Captain, which was hard to do while checking her suit's seals.

"Hey, Captain, wait up, please. I'm due to take Doc Julian out for a spin in this tomorrow. He's not been out in thirty years, and I've not flown in one of these for some time. I'd appreciate an opportunity to familiarise myself with the craft before I let Doc drive. Can I come with you, co-pilot?" Dollars was acting his best-excited schoolboy routine. He didn't want to let the guy know he was onto him. But the Captain wasn't going out alone.

"Really? The co-pilot completed her training solo. It's not going to do me any favours if my Indian counterpart completes her training alone, but I need my hand held!" She was clearly not happy.

"You'll be doing me a favour. This is for me, not you." Dollars gave it the puppy dog eyes.

"Sure, OK. Grab your suit." Was her grudging acquiescence. The puppy dog eyes always work, thought Dollars.

Dollars walked back and donned the half-suit he used. This protected his top half, his organic body against the vacuum.

But it left his lower half exposed. He stalked back into the departure lobby like a giant carnivorous bird of prey, his clawed metallic feet leaving slight gouges in the floor. Dollars was delighted to watch the fake 'technician' visibly twitch at the sight.

The technician finally spoke, "I'm not sure you can accompany the Captain. It's not logged. This is meant to be a solo flight." Dollars thought, 'Yeah, right.' The only reason they'd want her on her own is that she'd be easier to kill. It wasn't boasting, but Dollars was well aware that he was anything but easy to kill. He was going, or the Captain was staying. It was that simple.

"I've got a training mission in this tomorrow. I need to get my 'space legs,' he gave a leer at the technician at this point. There was a screeching sound as his left foot clawed the floor. It made everyone's teeth hurt. The 'Technician' paled slightly and took an involuntary step back. He was definitely not a real Tech. They were the 'gods of the lobbies.' They could stop anyone, and that was anyone, from leaving. If they didn't like the fit of the suit, you weren't going out – End Of! Even Dollar's dino-claws shouldn't have intimidated the Tech, if he was real.

"Ok, Captain, let's go." Said Dollars, walking past the 'Tech.' He had never even tried to check Dollar's suit. Another fail thought Dollars. They made their way through the airlock and out into the docked 'Lander.' Once securely seated, the Captain went through the flight checks. Dollars kept quiet so that no one would know he was also on board. He sent a quick message to his colleagues to pick up that 'Tech' and search for the real one. Hopefully, they'd find them still alive.

Someone had gone to considerable effort to kill the Captain, but which part of the trip would look most 'accidental'? There'd be an international outcry if they just murdered her. It had to look like an accident. They say that flying isn't dangerous. It's the landing. That would be it. Dollars relaxed. Nothing would happen until they began the landing sequence, so he settled back in his chair to enjoy the flight. The Captain was performing all the various training exercises. Low passes, manoeuvres. It would be she who flew the Landers down onto the surface of Callisto. After about two hours of training, control finally instructed the Captain to commence her landing approach. This was the most challenging part, anyway, even if your ship wasn't sabotaged.

He could hear her voice counting down the distance to the landing target and recording the speed of the approach. If it's going to happen, it'll be about now, thought Dollars.

"Engaging landing retros ... NOW!" The Captain was talking aloud, mainly for the benefit of the training crew. "Retros failure, repeat retros fail." Her voice was tight but still professional. Right, thought Dollars. Where would you cut something to make it look like a mechanical failure in the retros? The gas line.

"Helmet ON." Dollars said and made his way to the airlock. He knew the Captain was experienced enough to follow the standard practice, although, at this speed, nothing would protect them from the impact. He didn't have time to cycle the airlock and just hit the 'emergency blow.' The Cabin immediately depressurised, and he made his way through the double doors without slowing. His clawed feet gripped the handholds, and he made his way around the ship to the retro line housing, and yes, there it was, covered in crystals, where it had leaked as the Captain had tried to apply the jets.

Taking an emergency repair kit from the store on the hull of the ship, he opened the gas line housing and applied the repair. It instantly filled the recess with a foam that hardened in seconds. He looked over the side of the ship at the Moon's surface coming up towards them very fast.

They might not have those seconds.

He poked the foam, still soft. He counted to ten and did it again. He could hear the Captain's rapid breaths coming through the comms, but she was keeping quiet so as not to distract him. That couldn't be said for Control, who were yelling into his ears for an update.

Finally, the foam was so hard he couldn't dent it with his finger. Making his way towards the docking clamps, he spoke calmly into the radio, "Captain, hit the brakes. Retros are repaired. Captain, you're running out of road. Hit the BRAKES!"

"I can't. you're not back in the airlock." She sounded concerned for the first time.

"I'm fine. Hit the retros, NOW!" Dollars was looking over the side of the Lander. The Moon was fucking huge and close enough to touch.

His clawed feet gripped the docking clamps, and he hung on as several G's slammed into him. These docking clamps were designed to secure the ship and should be able to handle the forces, but they clearly weren't designed for this situation. A guy with prosthetic legs gripping on the outside while the craft performed an emergency landing was probably outside the design parameters. His legs would stay attached, no matter what, but whether he'd stay attached to his legs was another question.

This could be very messy.

The lander came down hard, the retros firing until it hit the ground. The landing struts absorbing the impact, but Dollars still felt the jarring run up his legs. The repair had held. It must have taken four whole seconds for the ship to descend. But to Dollars, it was at least an entire ice age. The craft slowly stopped vibrating, the dampeners soaking up the shock. As soon as the ship was still, Dollars made his way back into the lander and repressurised the cabin. Slowly removing the Captain's helmet, he asked, "You okay?"

She nodded, so Dollars confirmed with Control that the ship was down safely and that the Captain was uninjured. They'd still been shouting for an update all the way down. He understood their frustration, but sometimes he just wished they'd shut the fuck up!

Dollars turned off the comms. Now, they were completely alone.

"You really okay?" He asked again.

"What failed, the retros feed? Was it an accident?" Her voice was very cold.

"Nope, that Tech wasn't legit. He'd sabotaged the feedline and then made his way back into the lobby to ensure you got on the right trainer." Dollars was very businesslike. People had been trying to kill him for years.

"Was it one of the other women?" She asked, her tone almost conversational.

"Definitely not, this was your government. Your presence on this mission was an embarrassment to them. Didn't fit in with their isolationist rhetoric. Not only that, but sending a woman to do a man's job was an insult to their whole outlook." The last was delivered with a shrug.

"Thank you. I'd never have made it to the leak and back in time. I doubt anyone, but you could have stayed on the ship during the landing. Thank you." The Captain, now the tension was over, sagged with exhaustion. "I'm not used to people wanting to kill me. You look so calm."

Dollars just shrugged again, "Governments, terrorists, spies, and jealous husbands have been trying to kill me for years. This was just, well, a Tuesday for me." He grinned at her and was pleased to see the last had triggered a smile.

There was a slight jolt as the tractor towed the lander into alignment with the airlock so they could exit. As they made their way towards the door, Dollars added one final comment, "You'd better tell everyone it was just a fault. It will give my people more time to investigate."

Who his people were or what investigation they were engaged in wasn't clarified.

Chapter 8.

As the airlock opened, there were several people in the lobby. Some of the other crew had heard what had happened and had made their way to the airlock, some out of concern, others probably out of a sense of morbid curiosity. Charity and Isaiah Wilson both came through the door a moment later, and once they'd checked on the Captain, who was being poked and prodded by a Med Tech, much to her annoyance. They approached Dollars.

"Sabotage." Said Dollars in a low voice so only the other two could hear.

"The Americans? Do they know about the footprints?" Asked Isaiah.

"No. This was designed to remove the embarrassment of the Captain of the mission being one of their own. A martyr they could use, but a woman captaining the mission was just offensive to them on so many levels." He was smiling and looked cheerful, his facial expression belying his words. No one looking on would have thought anything was being discussed beyond some pleasant words about how much of a hero he was.

Another Tech approached the group and whispered into Dollar's ear, and then walked off and was lost in the hubbub.

"The fake Tech has disappeared, probably on one of the American Military bases already. The real Tech was found alive in his quarters. Someone had spiked his drink. Apart from a serious headache, he'll be fine. They've made their play. I wouldn't expect another attempt, but I'll increase security around the mission." Dollars looked pleased with himself.

...

Later that evening, Julian felt he ought to say something to the Captain regarding her near miss earlier in the day. But his feet felt like lead as he walked along the corridor despite the one-sixth gravity. His steps getting slower as he approached the Captain's quarters.

He stood in front of her door, instantly forgetting everything he'd planned to say, all the usual platitudes that one should say under the circumstances. Maybe he should have brought a card? A 'Sorry you were nearly killed in a spaceship crash!' card. His mind was spinning out of control.

His hand moved as if with a mind of its own, and he quietly tapped her door. He stood there terrified. What if she didn't answer, or even worse, what about if she did? She'd made her hostility towards him very clear. Maybe this was a mistake.

The door opened.

"Hi, I just came by to see how you were doing..." Julian ran out of words. The Captain was standing rigid in front of him. Her hands balled into fists, her knuckles white.

The Captain said nothing. She just stared at him. Her breathing laboured as though she'd been exercising. Or crying, Julian had no idea which.

He heard his wife's imagined voice in his mind – 'She needs a hug!' And he fell forwards as though a ghostly hand had pushed him. Initially, the Captain had tried to push him away. But then she clung to him, her nails cutting into the skin of his back, her whole body convulsing with silent tears. After a few moments of this, the Captain sighed, releasing the pent-up emotion of the day.

"Thank you for coming." Her words were very formal, her tone stilted. She stepped back into her quarters and shut the door without another word, leaving Julian standing in the empty corridor with a perplexed expression on his face.

...

Julian finally had the controls to himself. It was a low-gravity lander designed for

Lunar operations. It would be ideal for hopping around the Jupiter moons.

"How's it feeling?" Dollars was sitting in the co-pilot seat, looking very relaxed, especially after what had happened with the Captain the day before. Given the years since he'd last flown anything more powerful than an archaeologist's trowel, it had been decided that he would take Julian out for his first practice landing.

"Nice, a lot more responsive than I remember. It's like riding a bike, you never forget. The Lunar patrol runners didn't have this intuitive assist. you had to remember half of Newton's laws in your head as you went, or you'd end up flying backwards." Julian had a smile on his face for the first time in months. They were in micro-G, but the meds were working fine. He'd never had a problem with space sickness.

"Bring it around. Do you feel ready for a low-altitude pass over the training area?" Dollars asked. "You see the markers. There's also computer assistance on the screen. Can you bring it over and then down?" Dollars was calm, Julian was so excited his palms were sweating.

"Remember, Doc, if you scratch the paintwork, they'll take it out of your pay.

You could go all the way to Jupiter and still owe NASA money!" Dollars appeared to find this hilarious and sat sniggering.

Dollars checked with control that the training area was clear. Julian had sensed this wasn't a routine test landing and that something was likely to be thrown at him as a surprise. Dollars had started to grip his dual controls more than the light touch you'd normally have, and Julian thought any minute now.

Suddenly, all the lights went out on the control panel, and he was in free fall!

Shit, shit, shit – he thought, and then the training kicked back in. They'd done this to the new kids thirty years ago. He hit reset on the controls, glanced out the window to visibly check altitude, and touched the gas retros by instinct. The seat came up and hit him in the arse as the burst of gas slowed the craft. By the time he looked back at the panel, the controls were operating again, the reset had fixed the 'fault.'

"Nicely handled, Doc. I could tell you've done this before. There's no right way of passing the test. However, crapping yourself is normally a failure. The maintenance crew really hates it when that happens." Dollars was grinning, almost like a proud father. Catching Julian when he was still buzzing from the emergency scenario, Dollars said, "So what do you really think of the Captain?"

Julian stumbled over his adrenaline-filled words, "I know it's totally inappropriate. But I think she's beautiful. the colder she gets, the more I want her." Julian was startled by his own confession, having never put his feelings into words, not even to himself.

"You know you're on an open comms, right?" Stated the Captain, her words so cold, Julian wouldn't have been surprised to see ice forming around the speaker.

Chapter 9.

It had been two weeks since Dollars had caught Julian out by getting him to openly confess his feelings for the Captain. His relationship with all the other females had gone from frosty to zero Kelvin. Dollars had just laughed. He said he'd done him a favour by getting him to admit something to himself that was 'bleeding obvious' to everyone else, to quote Dollar's British accent.

Looking out of the shuttle's window, Julian could see the bulk of the Mars Liner getting closer. This, of course, was an optical illusion. It was them getting closer to the liner. The ship had been renamed 'Callisto' after one of the Jovian moons. It was on their itinerary. But seemed an odd name for the ship, but that wasn't his concern.

For the first time, the mission to Jupiter began to feel real. His time on the Lunar Training base had been something of a trip down memory lane. The Earth hung in the window. There were no political boundaries, just the one planet. The terminator was roughly halfway around the globe, half the world in sunlight, the other in darkness. He could make out the lights of Japan and the Pacific rim on the dark side, the shape of India. Then, with a jolt, he realised the large dark area Northeast of India, was what was left of China. Almost no lights were visible at all. 'America Reborn' had been very thorough. The scale of the loss of life was still hard to imagine, although, in this age of technology, every horrific moment was burned into his memory.

As they completed the transfer from the shuttle to the 'Callisto,' the airlock process took the longest part as they could only fit four in at a time. As they entered the main crew room, there was a surprise. They had expected various techs and other support crew, possibly even Charity, but not Isaiah Wilson, the Operations Mission Director.

The Captain appeared most concerned, even possibly resentful of his presence.

"Operations Director, are you coming with us?" The Captain had an odd expression on her beautiful face. It was, at least to Julian, a weird question. They had a few more days to check out the ship before departure. There wasn't any reason why he shouldn't be here.

"Welcome to the 'Callisto,' please drop off your gear in your marked rooms. I'm sure you're familiar with the ship layout by now. Meet me back here. Charity and I just wanted to say a few words before your departure." They all made their way to the various crew quarters. Julian, Dollars, and the Captain had single rooms. The other eight had to share. This might have been another cause of the low-bubbling resentment of the Captain. Dollars needed the extra space for his prosthetics and the various support equipment he needed. His bionic legs were a huge asset in space. But they required a lot of work to keep them running. The spares and other parts Dollars needed took up a lot of room. It hadn't been clear to Julian where Dollars ended and the legs began, but actually, they were more extensive than he'd thought. Dollars was metal from the waist down, not just legs but hip bone as well. But he could run faster and longer than average, and his feet could grip handholds, which was really handy in micro-G.

The Captain had her own quarters. Rank has its privileges, Dollar explained. But Julian thought, after what her people had done in China, it was more likely someone would smother her in her sleep if she shared with anyone else. Julian also had his own room. It hadn't been said in so many words, but he couldn't share a room with anyone else.

He was male!

The religious commentators in the US had screamed about the moral implications of a man on a ship full of women. There were times when Julian was very glad he was Canadian.

...

The Main crew room was tense. The Captain had a clear chip on her shoulder. Whether it was him or just the refusal of the male gender generally to spontaneously combust wasn't apparent. The other eight women had split up into cliques. Charity and Director Wilson were both looking at each other, like they had a secret they weren't sure how to break. The only person who was happy and relaxed, 'chipper', to use his description, was Dollars. He looked like he knew exactly what was coming and was just waiting for the fireworks.

Director Isaiah Wilson called the room to order with the words, "I need to explain to you the real reason behind this mission."

"The Jovian survey probe found these on the surface of Callisto. As you can see from the image, they look like footprints. Who left them and how long ago is the real reason for this mission and the rushed time scale. There's the possibility that whoever or whatever left those footprints could still be on Callisto, or they could have been left four billion years ago. It's your mission to find out." Director Wilson stood in front of the large display panel and waited for the reaction. Given how emotionally unstable some of them were, Julian thought there might be a mutiny. If it hadn't been such a rush to hit the launch window, Julian doubted any of them would have been kept on the mission. But now the rush and his reason for being here all made a lot of sense.

Oddly, the Captain appeared relieved, "I knew something was very wrong with this whole set-up. Now it's clear: I couldn't understand the need for a tactical officer on a mission to Jupiter, nor the presence of a palaeontologist. Frankly, I thought I was getting paranoid. I'm relieved to know that there really was a conspiracy. I'm assuming Dollars knew?" The Captain sat down heavily in a chair. But her feelings were not shared by many of the others.

"There might be aliens on Callisto. Are you mad? Those footprints are obviously faked. A trip to Jupiter, a chance to go down in history. But chasing after aliens. We'll be laughing stocks." The Swiss Med Tech was incredulous.

Director Wilson tried to be reassuring, "The mission to Jupiter will be exactly what you signed up for. The new insights into the

Jovian system will give us a real boost in understanding how the gas giant formed and the resources that could be used by future missions, possibly even permanent habitats. The possibility of aliens visiting Callisto is, and will remain, a closely guarded secret until you've confirmed their authenticity. I don't need to tell you about the political repercussions for the US, as well as the cultural impact worldwide. No one beyond this room and a few security personnel know the real reason for the mission."

"If the aliens are still there and are hostile?" Asked the astronaut from France, her accent distinctive.

"Boom." This was Dollars jumping in, "That's where I come in. If the aliens are long gone, then Doc will get to do his fossil thing. If they are still there and friendly, the Captain can negotiate with them. If they're hostile flesh-eating monsters, then that's my problem. As I said, 'Boom'."

...

Operations Director Isaiah Wilson was relieved the 'reveal' had gone better than expected. The Captain appeared genuinely happy to have understood the true reason for the mission. The rushed time scale and the secrecy, the sense that she was the only one to feel the weird vibe of the whole arrangement, must have weighed heavily on her mind. The women's resentment of 'The Man' was understandable. Even an organisation such as NASA couldn't ignore the political pressure completely. The chauvinistic, ultra-right, religious nuts had been in power now for more than twenty years. You couldn't 'pray-away' climate change any more than you could influence someone's sexual preferences – But it didn't stop them from trying. They would have closed down the space program if they could, but it made too much money.

Understandably, the female crew members resented living in a society that treated women as worse than second-class. To quote that campaigner who had gone into hiding after receiving death threats. "The US has gone totally – 'Handmaid's Tale'."

...

"You will have a secure direct comms to my office. I will be your point of contact for any matters relating to the 'Footprints'. Routine communications will be carried out in the normal way. But it's anticipated that once you get to Callisto, you'll need to send regular encrypted transmissions. Charity, I, or assigned security personnel will be available twenty-four-seven. It's a long way to Jupiter, but you'll be in hibernation for most of it. Any questions? If you've got any last-minute items to discuss, please bring those to Charity's attention. I'm going to leave shortly. Too much time up here will start to raise eyebrows ground-side. So, I'll be leaving in a few minutes. Charity and the Techs will be with you until the final checks. Good luck." Isaiah Wilson finished his little speech and, with a nod to Charity and then to Dollars, made his way towards the Airlock for the return to Texas.

No one even moved to thank him or say their goodbyes. They were all just too overwhelmed by the revelation that they might be going to meet aliens on Callisto.

..

The next few days were taken up with final checks. Dollars had his people crawling all over the place, looking for anything 'wrong'. However, no one other than Charity even knew they weren't just normal Techs being extra diligent.

The hibernation pods, 'Coffins', had been their nickname for the last decade since they were first developed. They were sometimes used on the Asteroid runs, where the reduced air and food, along with the reduced distress to the small crew, made a difference. But their resemblance to 'your last resting place' was very unpleasant. Some had suggested that they should be transparent, but the thought of people seeing your 'resting bitch face' for months on end wasn't popular either. So 'Coffins' they remained.

The run out to Mars would be 'Awake'. Almost all of the crew wanted to see the planet close up. They'd use gravity assist to accelerate the ship for the journey to Jupiter. After Mars, they'd be in their 'coffins' for months, waking only for Med checks and then back to sleep.

The run to Mars would take a few months, and the trip to the Jovian system would take a few years. But it wouldn't actually feel like more than a week. Over the whole journey from Mars to Jupiter, they'd be awake for barely a week, subjectively. The three droids would handle the ship. Even the Captain sleeping along with the rest of the crew. Julian was painfully aware that he was little more than cargo until they got to Callisto.

...

Julian watched as the last Techs squeezed into the airlock, leaving only Charity in the crew room of the Liner.

"I had planned a speech for this point, but anything I say is going to feel hollow. I wish I could give you all a big hug." She had a tear in the corner of her eye. Julian felt embarrassed for her. He'd never been great at these sorts of situations. Some of the other women looked equally upset, but most still had the hard edge to them they'd had all along. It was unfair to criticise Charity for her country's government's actions. But that didn't stop them from doing it.

Julian moved forward and reached out his hand, but Charity grabbed him and pulled him in for a bear hug. She was a little taller than him and was incredibly strong. She squeezed until he couldn't breathe.

Then, without another word, she walked into the airlock. She nodded to Dollars as the doors closed, and that was that. They were alone.

"Is there a drive-through on the way to Mars? I fancy a burger." Said Dollars with a grin.

The Captain told everyone to take their assigned positions. For Julian, that was his bunk. Unless the pilots were incapacitated, there was nothing for him to do until they got to Callisto. As Julian lay on his bunk reading, he felt the vibration of the engines start their de-orbital burn. They were on their way.

...

There was a knock at Julian's door, opening it, he found Dollars standing there, tool bag in hand, like he'd come to fix a dripping tap.

"You busy?" Dollars asked, walking into the room, even before Julian had a chance to invite him in. The room was large by spaceship standards but still felt cramped with the two of them in there. Dollars just stood staring at Julian like he was gauging his reaction to a question he hadn't asked yet.

"Busy?" Dollars asked again.

"You know I'm not. Why? What's the tool bag for?" Julian gestured in its direction.

"Got a little job for you. Some orientation training, at least that's what we're going to call it." Dollars tapped the side of his nose knowingly.

He might know what was going on, but Julian was totally in the dark. "What do you want me to do, fix a dripping tap?"

"Nope, I want you to check and see if the ship has been sabotaged." Dollars was dead calm, very businesslike. This made his words even scarier. He was serious; Julian must have gaped because Dollars reached out and flicked his chin, closing his mouth.

"You saw my people crawling all over the ship before we left?"

"I saw technicians checking the ship before we left orbit. I didn't know they were yours as such, I assumed they all worked for NASA. I did notice that there were two teams and that they didn't get on well with each other, which I thought was odd." Julian explained, recalling his feelings at the time.

"Well, yes, some worked for NASA, and some worked for me, well it's kind of complicated. The NASA team wasn't happy as they thought the other crew was checking up on them, and no one likes that; they were checking for sabotage. That training flight was the one where the Captain nearly crashed. It was sabotage; someone cut her gas line to the retros. If I hadn't been there, she'd have hit the moon so hard, it would have rung like a bell." Dollars was still very calm, expressing little emotion. Julian felt himself swallow; his mouth had gone dry.

"I didn't know..." His voice ran down. Now he understood the Captain's reaction when he'd gone to see her after the near crash. A faulty unit would have made her angry, but to know that someone wanted to kill you so much that they'd sabotage a spacecraft must have terrified her, not even knowing who she could trust. She must have felt so alone and vulnerable.

Dollars looked at him as though his thoughts had been written across his face. "So, I need you to check over the ship; we'll tell everyone that I'm giving you training in emergency repairs. But the real reason is that I need someone looking for anything that my techs missed. The Captain is too busy, and I'm too noticeable. But no one cares what you do. Sorry, I care, but you know the way things are. You are the one person I can trust. Frankly, I'm not entirely sure about the Captain, to be honest. But I doubt she's the martyr type."

"She was terrified and so upset, you know, after the near crash during training. I can't imagine she staged that." Julian said.

"Oh, yes, I forgot you went to see her." Dollars replied.

"You know?"

"Everyone knows, there are cameras everywhere, mate. So, you gonna help me? Take these tools, and check every panel, cubbyhole, recess and crevice you can think of."

Julian nodded and found his hand reaching out and taking the heavy tool bag, even before his brain had decided what to do. He spent the next few weeks nosing around the ship and getting in everyone's way but found nothing. Dollars had also been checking, but he'd been a lot more discrete. If there had been a saboteur on board, they would have been watching for Dr Julian Richards. They wouldn't have seen Dollars at all. But in reality, neither of them found anything amiss. Whether that meant there was nothing to find or it was just very well hidden wasn't entirely clear; Dollar's paranoia had begun to infect Julian. The one part of the ship Dollars had told Julian he didn't need to check was a couple of storage containers that had just appeared; they didn't have the usual NASA stickers. They had arrived as though by magic. How Dollars smuggled them past the NASA Techs was another mystery. Dollars hovered around them like a mother hen. What they contained was just one more thing Julian didn't know. It was a long list!

...

The translucent lid of his coffin was too close to his face. Julian could feel a tightness in his chest and the familiar difficulty in catching his breath. He'd always had a problem with claustrophobia, but fortunately, once the 'coffin' was switched on, he'd be asleep. The Swiss Med Tech Sofia opened the lid and asked, "Comfortable?"

It was apparent from her tone that she really didn't care either way. They'd been trying out the hibernation units. They did this as a way of desensitising themselves to them.

Dollars walked past the door to the sleep chamber, "Hey Dollars, wait up." Julian jumped out of the pod and nearly slipped. The ship's gravity still didn't feel right somehow.

"I've been meaning to ask, can you fit in the sleep unit with your legs, okay?" asked Julian.

"Yes, they fold up pretty small when not needed. I fit in my 'Coffin'. I just hope someone doesn't drive a stake through my heart while I'm sleeping." He gave a very fake vampiric laugh.

...

There was a tension on the ship. It was palpable; you could have cut it, even with the plastic cutlery! Julian sat in the main dining lounge. It had mirrors and screens around and was designed in such a way as to give the feeling of openness, although, of course, in the very finite confines of a spaceship, it was small by terrestrial standards. The Captain entered the lounge and stood, momentarily looking around the half-filled room for a convenient space, but all the tables were busy. There was plenty of space in reality, but at the sight of the Captain, there was a hush and shuffling. The tables and chairs were held to the floor by powerful electromagnets. If you wanted to move them, you had to hold a button underneath and then move the chair or table. Upon releasing the button, the magnet instantly held it to the floor. There was a series of audible clicks and scrapes as somehow the room transformed. Suddenly, there were no available chairs, no one looked at her, no welcoming nods, just cold distrust and an almost insolent refusal to even acknowledge her presence.

To some degree, it was normal for no one to socialise with the Captain; she was their boss, but that wasn't the reason. She was American, and that was enough for many – After what her government had done in China, a few of the crew might have been happy to shove her out of an airlock.

Julian wasn't treated much better; he was a man – The closest thing to the Patriarchy available, and so was treated with some hostility by a few of the women. The exception to this was Maria; maybe it was because she was Brazilian, but she always had a more cheerful outlook. She would sometimes try to talk to Julian, but the attitude of the other women discouraged her. Julian had felt on occasion that there was a subtext to her comments, but he'd never understood what it was.

Dollars was, of course, the life and soul, regaling the women with stories of his daring do. Although he was male, his prosthetics gave him a sympathy vote that overshadowed his gender.

Julian looked up and nodded to the Captain; his table had become the only one available, the single chair on his table the only chair in the room that wasn't suddenly 'busy'. He made a discrete hand gesture, barely noticeable to anyone but the Captain, as, of course, everyone else was terribly busy with something important. There was no exchange of words, but somehow, Julian came to look forward to these forced interactions.

Just occasionally, Julian would look up from his meal or from reading and catch the

Captain looking at him, a look of bemusement on her face.

...

The three-month journey from Earth orbit to the Mars slingshot was over surprisingly fast. Julian had spent the first few weeks playing at being a secret agent. After that, he'd fallen into a more normal routine. Reading up on the ship's procedures and the reports on Jupiter, and especially Callisto, took much of his day. He wasn't much more than cargo for this part of the journey. The Med Techs were doing constant medical assessments to ensure everyone was staying fit. It wasn't like the old days without gravity; Julian had to do his runs around the ship's gravity areas. Maintaining bone and muscle wasn't so much of a problem; radiation, however, was always a danger, but 'Solar Storm' drills ensured that they were as ready as they could be. The ship's flight crew had been doing various tests of the systems, including the Droids. They had to test everything as thoroughly as possible. If something was wrong, they could stay at Mars until it was repaired, but once they left Mars orbit, they were effectively on their own.

The lunch times were the worst, although, in space, there was no night or day; the ship maintained a basic Earth Day schedule. The day divided into two shifts of twelve hours. The Captain and the Swiss Med Tech, along with other crew members, took one shift. Maria, the other Med Tech, and the Co-pilot, along with the remaining crew, took the other shift. Julian was assigned to the Captain's team, shift One as it was known, even this created tension, implying that the other shift was second best.

This meant that Julian rarely saw Maria but did spend most lunch breaks with the Captain. Dollars switched from one team to another as the mood took him. Dollars was a rule unto himself – 'God moves in mysterious ways.' It was one of his favourite lines whenever Julian asked about it. His ego knew no bounds.

As none of the crew wanted to spend time with Julian or with the Captain most lunchtimes, they sat together. Julian had tried on a few occasions to talk with the Captain, but the look he got was so cold that it made him check that the environmental controls were working okay. Over the months from Earth to Mars, however, the sheer isolation made the Captain relent. Although they wouldn't call their lunchtime rendezvouses romantic, it was the high point of Julian's day, and just sometimes he'd catch the Captain staring at him. There was almost a smile on her face. Maybe, just maybe, they'd become the high point of her day, too.

Chapter 10.

Mars was huge. Even through the large viewing window, you couldn't see the whole planet. They were too close. The ship was barely skimming the atmosphere. The observation room was located in the central core and, therefore, had no gravity. But that didn't prevent almost everyone from piling in to watch the Mars fly-by.

Julian stared at the planet, its reflected red glow filling the room. The light giving everyone's faces a demonic tinge. The polar caps were visible, and Olympus Mons was on the horizon, its tip catching the sunlight.

Julian had a vision of what the world must have looked like billions of years before, with blue oceans reflecting the sunlight and wispy clouds scudding across the sky. Could there once have been ships sailing that world-girdling ocean?

A few of the more knowledgeable members of the crew were pointing out the various features of the surface as they skimmed past the window. Beyond Olympus Mons, Julian didn't know a lot of them himself and listened in rapt attention as key landmarks were identified. Even the ever-cynical Dollars enjoyed the awe-inspiring majesty of this once-in-a-lifetime trip.

"You ever been to Mars?" Julian asked him in a hushed voice.

"Nope, never have, been to the Moon a few times. But not Mars." Even Dollars was subdued in the presence of such an incredible view.

After barely forty-five minutes, Mars started to recede from the viewing window and then was gone.

The ship was now beginning the long run to Jupiter.

...

"Team two, six hours to hibernation, six hours to hibernation." The Captain's voice was audible throughout the ship. Julian made his way to his quarters and began tidying his things. The liner was a hive of activity after the pause to watch Mars glide past now; the ship needed to be prepared for the run to Jupiter. Everything had to be secured. The vessel could perform manoeuvres while they were asleep. It was important that nothing was loose or could fall over.

The eight crew of team two stood in a row outside the Hibernation Suite. Dollars was there. He was also on team two and nodded to Julian. He, like Julian, was little more than cargo on this part of the mission and was feeling the weight of time pressing down on him. He was bored. No one had tried to kill anyone for weeks, and he was feeling useless. Julian had been reading everything he could on Callisto. But even he was feeling a bit lost.

Some of the women had formed close relationships with their bunkmates and hugged each other as they were helped into the sleep units by a Med Tech and a droid. From the way some kissed, they'd become more than just friends in the past three months. Dollars wandered over to watch as Julian was 'put to sleep' although he instantly wished that thought hadn't crossed his mind as the 'Coffin' lid was closed. The droid having connected the various pipes to him, along with the stim-pads, before discreetly pulling the sheet up over his naked body.

"Sleep well Doc. You want me to read you a bedtime story… " Were Dollar's last words as the hibernation unit was switched on, and Julian's world drifted into darkness.

The ship began the 30-month voyage to Jupiter, inhabited only by the sleeping crew in dreamless hibernation.

Chapter 11.

(Month - 7.5 of 30)

The droid was holding up the coffin lid and staring down at him, her, or rather, its face blank and expressionless. Julian tried hard not to scream.

His whole body ached. He slowly removed the stim-pads and tried to get out. The droid reached down and carefully removed all the pipes from his private parts. It felt weird to have a woman, DROID, touch him. But it was just a droid – an IT, rather than a HER.

He sniffed himself, he stunk. "How long?" he croaked out.

"Seven months and fourteen days." Was the bland response.

Julian slid out of the unit and staggered towards the bathroom. He needed to pee – 'au naturel', so to speak. He stuck his head in the medical room and saw Maria, the Brazilian Med Tech, and one of the crew going through the various health checks. He nodded and pointed to the shower room.

After the shower, he felt better. Drinking a large cup of water, he walked back into the medical unit, his legs still wobbly. Thirty-six hours awake, food and water in, waste out, and then back to sleep.

"Why does everything hurt?" Julian asked the Med as they were going through the checks.

"We're pushing the hibernation units to the limits. Three to six months is best, but who wants to spend more than needed staring at the walls of this tin can." The Med Tech was clearly in no better shape than he was.

...

(Month - 15 of 30)

Again, the droid looked down at him, and he tried not to scream. It just had a whole 'horror movie' vibe about it. The bland, emotionless, genderless face stared down at his helpless naked body. It just creeped him out. If possible, his body felt even worse than the last time.

Through the same routine, food, drink, med checks and then back to sleep.

...

(Month - 22.5 of 30)

This time, the Med tech was looking down at him. The droid stood, holding the lid, but was not, mercifully, staring blankly into his eyes. He knew it had something to do with pupil dilations, but it gave him nightmares.

"Hi Dr Julian, how are you feeling." The Med Tech Maria asked. Her Brazilian Portuguese accent always sounded like she was laughing at someone, and Julian felt like it was probably him.

"How long?" Julian croaked.

"Another seven and a half months, less than a year to go. I got fed up with you screaming every time the droid opened your sleep unit, so I thought I'd do it myself. I'm flattered to note that you didn't scream at the sight of me looking down into your face. Although having looked in the mirror, I'm not sure why. I look awful." She smiled down at him and winked. She had a sense of humour, unlike her Swiss counterpart. Maybe it was a national stereotype, but she had all the personality of one of her nation's famous watches.

"Thanks," was about all Julian could manage. One more sleep, then Jupiter. It reminded him of being a kid – How many sleeps till Christmas?

Chapter 12.

(Month – 28.5 of 30)

"Dr Julian, wake up, ... Medical ... Captain... Wake up. Dr Julian Richards, wake up, the Captain is ... incapacitated. Repeat. Medical incident the ... Isolation Psychosis ... Captain is ... Wake up, Dr Richards. Julian, wake up, for FUCKS SAKE!

Julian was awake.

Charity's voice was screaming in his ears. He sat up suddenly and struck his head on the inside of his hibernation unit. Everything spun around for a moment, but eventually, his eyes focused. The droids had made opening the lids look easy. It wasn't. His muscles were shaking and weak. He could barely lift it. As he slipped out, he realised that parts of him were still attached, so he removed the various pipes. It hurt a lot more when he did it. The droids managed it without too much pain. He didn't!

The air in the room smelt wrong, stale food smells filled the ship. This wasn't good. First stop bathroom. After that, he made his way along the main corridor towards the control room. There was a droid lying face down on the floor; it didn't look damaged, so he left it. The first thing to check was the control room and ascertain they weren't about to slam straight into something. The stale food smell got worse, along with the smell of stale sweat. As he entered the control room, he saw the remaining two droids. Both were deactivated. There was nothing on the screens to indicate an immediate problem, so he switched the first droid back on. It sat there for a few moments as it initialised.

"What happened?" Julian asked. He wasn't sure why he was whispering, but it seemed fitting.

"The Captain deactivated me. She used security overrides, but I don't understand why. I fear the Captain might be unwell." The Droid's emotionless voice was spooky. Julian was unsettled enough without the droid to add to his fears.

"Check the ship and the systems. I'll wake up the other droid. Once it's fully initialised, send it to check on the sleeping crew. I'll look for the Captain." Julian was feeling a bit more confident now he had something positive to do. Beyond creeping around what had felt like the Mary Celeste.

Julian examined the comms unit; it had been turned off, and he didn't have either the clearance or the knowledge to turn it back on. The med-channel was still working so Ground Control would know he was awake.

Where was the Captain? – Following the smell appeared to be the best approach.

Julian walked carefully along the corridor in the direction of the main crew lounge. This was definitely the source of the smells: both stale food and staler human.

He walked in the door, not sure what to expect. The Captain was throwing food about the room, ripping open the packets, and spraying the contents around the floor.

Charity had said something about 'isolation psychosis' – What that was exactly and how to treat it were not something he had even the first guess about. But throwing food around might have been a symptom. The room smelled awful; the Captain's hair was matted down, and her clothes were covered in food and other stains Julian didn't even want to think about.

At the sight of him, she screamed and started to throw the food at him. She must have been rational enough to deactivate the primary comms so Control couldn't reactivate the droids remotely. There was no easy way of switching off the med feeds from the hibernation pods. This enabled Charity to reach him. But now the Captain was behaving like a monkey in a zoo and throwing food at anyone it didn't like, which, at the moment, was him.

"Captain, can you hear me?" Julian asked.

More food and more screaming, he could try and wake up a Med Tech, could they give her something? He retreated from the room for a few moments and found the third droid. Switching it back on, he waited until it was fully responsive.

"Treatment for 'isolation psychosis'?" Julian asked the droid. They should know almost everything.

"Isolation Psychosis' is the name given to a medical condition that can affect certain people who become physically isolated. People stranded for long periods in a remote location can develop various coping mechanisms. Sometimes, these can distort the person's awareness of the world around them-" Julian interrupted the droid with another question.

"What's the cure?"

"There is no immediate cure. The patient usually requires considerable therapy to be able to function normally-"

"Ok, that's enough. Please check on the sleeping crew and work with your colleagues to reestablish comms. The ship needs a thorough check. How long have you been offline?" Julian needed to understand the time the Captain had been on her own.

"Eight days, thirteen hours and twenty-seven minutes." Was the bland reply.

The Captain had been awake for eight days. They were the furthest any human had ever been from Earth, they were only weeks away from Jupiter. She was the only crew member awake on a ship further into space than anyone had ever gone. She was the most isolated person in history. No wonder her mind had shattered.

Taking a deep breath, Julian made his way back into the crew lounge. But the Captain wasn't there.

He heard a woman shouting and the emotionless replies of the droids. The Captain was trying to switch them back off. But now she was too far gone to remember the security overrides. He ran in the direction of the voices and, turning a corner, ran straight into the Captain. They both collided and fell to the floor. The Captain screamed at him again but was out of ammo. There was no food around to throw at him.

Julian staggered to his feet. He had not fully recovered from hibernation and was still a bit shaky. The Captain was rubbing her head where they'd collided. She looked at him in growing recognition.

"Dr Julian Richards, are you okay? Why are you awake?" The Captain asked.

"Control woke me up because you were unwell," Julian replied as if talking to a frightened child.

"Unwell, what was wrong with me, and why didn't they contact a Med Tech?" She asked in alarm.

All good questions, thought Julian. It's a shame he didn't have any good answers. Usually, someone would be beyond any medical help if you needed a Palaeontologist.

"I don't know why they woke me up. Once we speak to Control, I'm sure they can explain it." Julian was relieved that the Captain had started to function normally.

"What's that awful smell?" She asked next.

"I'm sorry to report, but I think it's you." Said Julian with an embarrassed shrug.

Chapter 13.

Julian walked with the Captain to the showers and stood waiting just outside for her. She begged him not to leave her alone. So, he stood outside, making small talk. She took some time. It was obvious she hadn't washed in days.

"Julian?" She called from in the shower.

"Yes, it's okay. I'm still outside. You're not alone." Julian reassured. He'd still been speaking. Maybe she couldn't hear him over the noise of the shower.

"Julian?" She called again. This time, her tone was more urgent, desperate. So, he felt he had no choice but to walk into the shower. He feared she'd have a relapse if she was alone. The Captain just stood naked in the shower. The water turned off. Her arms were at her side, her fists clenched. She just stared at him. She was scared but also looked ready to fight.

"Julian?" She said again, her voice trembling and uncertain.

Julian heard the imagined voice of his wife in his mind, for the first time since he'd left the Moon, saying, 'She needs you'. There was the sound of a door closing, and he knew he'd never imagine hearing his wife's voice in his head again. He had given himself permission to move on.

"Are you sure you want this?" Julian asked, feeling awkward. He hadn't been intimate with a woman since his wife. The Captain just nodded, her body tense with the fear of rejection.

Julian removed his clothes, stepped into the shower, and took the Captain in his arms. They were both awkward and self-conscious at first. But they started to relax and began massaging and washing each other down.

They made their way, still naked, to the Captain's room. As she closed the door, she clung to Julian. She appeared so insecure, desperate for his reassurance.

"It's okay, Captain. Everything will be okay. You're never going to be alone again." Julian whispered in her ear.

"Please call me Abi."

Julian lowered her onto her bed, and Julian and Abi made love.

Chapter 14.

As Julian awoke, he could feel Abi gripping onto him as if her life depended on it. Slowly and carefully so as to not wake her, Julian climbed out of bed and made his way to the ship's bridge via the bathroom, to check in on the droids. One was recharging, and the other two were in the pilot's seats.

"Please report," Julian asked.

The closest droid then began a long list of all the ship's systems that had been checked, there was nothing that caused Julian concern. More importantly, there was nothing the droids were concerned about either. After all, they knew this ship far better than he did.

"Comms are working?" Julian wanted to double-check.

"Yes, comms are working. There are 73 pending messages marked 'Urgent'." The droid stated.

Julian could only imagine the stress this had caused back Earthside.

"You've sent a report confirming the Captain's health has improved and that the ship's systems are operational?" Julian asked.

But before the droid had had a chance to do more than say yes, the Captain's terrified scream shattered the peace of the ship. Julian ran, one of the droids right behind him. His late wife had been scared of spiders, but he hadn't seen any on the ship. Maybe an eight-legged monster was creeping across the Captain's floor.

"Abi, it's okay. I'm coming," Julian called, struggling to catch his breath as he ran.

Entering her room, he looked around for the spider, but nothing was scuttling across her floor. Abi was sitting up in bed, her face white. She was utterly terrified. At the sight of him, the sobs started; all Julian could do was take her in his arms.

"I thought I was alone. I thought last night was just a dream." Her whole body was convulsing. Her tears staining his shirt. Julian held her and stroked her hair, whispering reassurances in her ear.

The droid stood in the doorway for a few moments and then slipped back out. This was something that Julian could handle.

"I just went to the bathroom and checked on the droids. I thought you could do with the sleep." Julian said.

"Sorry, I thought I was alone again; I was so scared." Was her reply between sobs.

"It's going to be okay. I'm never going to leave you. Where am I going to go, I can't exactly walk home?" He smiled into her eyes, and she grinned back.

"After I've gone to the bathroom, can we go back to bed for a few minutes?" She asked.

"I hope I can last longer than only a few minutes." He joked and was pleased to see her smile. "Although we're going to need to prepare a detailed report for Ground Control, the droids have sent an update. But Earthside are going to want to receive a video report from us in person."

Abi looked embarrassed, "Are we going to need to tell them everything?"

"No, but I think I know why they woke me up. It takes about six days for the hibernation wake-up cycle to complete. I might have been next in the sequence for a routine wake-up. But my guess is that Charity from HR decided we needed some 'human relations'." As he finished talking, he lunged for her.

She squealed and ran for the toilet. He watched her scamper naked across the room.

Chapter 15.

For Captain Abi Thomas and Julian, the following weeks became an unexpected honeymoon. Neither would have imagined that was even possible, Abi facing life alone because of the choices she'd made and those forced upon her. Julian never imagined he could even love again.

Ground Control felt that it would be medically unwise for the Captain to return to hibernation for the last few weeks of the journey. The fact that she screamed and cried, even at the thought of it, was a good indication that another solution needed to be found. Despite the Captain's one-person food fight, there was no shortage of supplies, so they could just stay awake until Jupiter.

The following morning, Abi and Julian were sitting in the dining room eating.

"How's your head?" Julian asked, looking at the large bump.

"It hurts, yours? She replied gingerly, touching the spot in question.

"There's something I want to ask, to talk with you about ... " Julian ran down, unsure how to broach the subject.

The Captain looked at him wryly, a grin beginning to form.

"Are you worried about us having sex? Do you think you've taken advantage of a vulnerable woman? Are you feeling guilty?" She was now smiling, trying hard not to laugh.

All Julian could do was mumble out. "Yes, well, kind of. I felt that we had a connection, those meals together on the flight out to Mars, even during that time on the Luna training base. But you've always avoided any form of physical contact; I just wanted to be sure this is what you wanted."

Julian looked straight into Abi's eyes, trying to gauge her real feelings.

"Yes, this," Gesturing to the two of them, "Is really what I want." She took a deep breath before continuing.

"My life has been so tightly controlled; I've had to bury my feelings, my devout religious upbringing, and then the astronaut training. Any suggestion of immorality, of sin, would have blocked those career paths for me. You know sex outside of marriage is punishable by death, right? Although it doesn't normally happen, I'd never have been allowed to be an astronaut if there was even a hint of anything immoral. I'd have been considered a 'bad role model'. My father's position got me in the door of the astronaut training, but it could never have protected me. So, kids, marriage just wasn't going to be possible for me, and before you ask, no women either – That's considered unnatural and would have gotten me locked in a re-education camp for sure. You know I had to have my virginity confirmed by a nurse every 3 years?" Abi stopped and took a drink of her coffee, before continuing.

"But when I was in the shower, I realised that all those people that had controlled me are gone or are half a billion miles away. My mum died just before the training started. Otherwise, I wouldn't have come. My father had died a few years ago."

Julian mumbled about how sorry he was; he reached out and grasped her hand.

"What could Richmond do to me out here, sack me, put me on trial? We don't know what we'll find on Callisto; there's a fair chance we'll never make it home, so why worry about a trial? Anyway, maybe I could stay on Mars or Lunar; I'm an experienced astronaut, I'm sure I can get a job somewhere. So, when I was standing in the shower, it all seemed to fall into place – Why was I living a life imposed on me by my parents, my government and by a religion that I'm not sure I believe any more? When outside the shower door was a man who loved me." She finished with a sob, and Julian squeezed her hand again.

They sat there holding hands and tried to eat between the tears.

...

Julian and Abi were busy with the system checks and astronomical observations. But they almost never spent more than a few moments apart; they were inseparable.

"What does Abi stand for? Is It short for something?" Julian asked one evening as they were sitting at the dining table in the crew lounge. The droids having cleaned the area thoroughly, so that not even a trace of the foul smell remained.

"Abishag." She replied, the look on her face making it very clear that laughter would get him thrown out of an airlock. "It's biblical. My family are very religious, even before that was a legal requirement. My Father's high rank in the church helped to clear away some of the obstacles to my qualifying as an astronaut once the 'Reborn' people took charge."

"It was a little joke I had with myself, a sick joke, really. I changed it to 'Abi-no-shag'. It was a more fitting name. Although it's no longer true." She smiled and, reaching across the table, squeezed Julian's hand.

Regardless of what they found on Callisto – although it might have taken several years and half a billion miles, they had found love.

Chapter 16.

It was finally time for the rest of the crew to awaken. There was a schedule for the revivals, in order of priority; those required to navigate were first, along with the Med Techs, and those whose roles were mostly on the surface would be last. Julian and Abi's honeymoon cruise was over. Their 'couple' status now widely known and greeted with varying responses. Some were jealous, either of Julian or of the Captain, depending on their personal preferences. Some were just angry that the Captain even deserved happiness, as though her personal suffering could in some way atone for the crimes of the American Government.

The ship was all activity again after weeks of stillness. The droids assisting the Med Techs to awaken the crew. The bathroom and showers were in constant use. Julian was pleased to hear the clicking of Dollar's metallic legs as he walked along the main corridor. They shook hands, and Dollars asked him what had happened.

"Why do you think something's happened?" Julian was perplexed.

"Firstly, you're awake before me. That's out of sequence. Secondly, you've got a stupid grin on your face. And I'm not that good looking that it's just you've missed me. And thirdly, I overheard you just refer to the Captain as Abi. Even I'm not allowed to do that. So, talk!"

Julian recounted the events that had occurred after he'd been awoken by Ground Control. Leaving out the more personal connections he'd had with the Captain.

"Okay, so reading between the lines, filling in all the juicy stuff that you're too much of a gentleman to boast about. You might study fossils, but I'm pleased to see you're not fossilised yourself. And given you're a geologist, I hope you were able to get ROCK hard for her." Dollars slapped Julian on the back, laughing at his own jokes.

"Dollars, who are you really? I mean – John Williams – 'Like the composer.'" They both said the last simultaneously. "You rescued the Captain, Abi, and then the next day took me on a training flight like nothing had happened. You appear to know everything that's going on. Back on Moon base I saw guys come up to you and whisper to you and then just disappear. Even the senior people at NASA defer to you. Who are you really?"

Dollars looked at him and grinned. He actually appeared impressed that Julian had spotted all this going on. He hadn't, the

Captain had. Julian didn't have a clue. But he wasn't going to say that...

"That Abi is very observant." He said thoughtfully. Then, in a fake Scottish accent, he continued, "My name is Williams, John Williams. At your service." Dollars gave a little bow. He turned on his metallic heals and marched smartly away, whistling the theme music from the old James Bond films, not the new Disney remakes.

Julian had finally started to understand the enigma that was Captain Abi Thomas. But this mission had plenty more mysteries.

Who left the footprints?

What were they going to find on Callisto?

Who, or what, was Dollars really, apart from being awful at whistling?

Chapter 17.

The 'Callisto' needed to reduce speed. It had been coasting along since sling-shotting around Mars. That momentum would be reduced in two ways. As the ship had reached the halfway point, it had flipped around so that the main engines pointed towards Jupiter rather than the Sun. They would begin to reduce the ship's speed. But the main brake was Jupiter itself. Using the same sling-shot technique they had used to accelerate, they would now use to slow down.

The Captain and Copilot were at their controls, almost all the rest of the crew were staring out of the viewing windows. They would spiral around Jupiter several times, bleeding off speed as they went. Once the correct speed had been achieved, they'd leave Jupiter and enter orbit around the moon Callisto.

What awaited them on Callisto? The crew's anticipation was palpable as they prepared to uncover the mysteries of the moon.

Chapter 18.

The surface of Callisto was bright in the viewing window. Although the Sun was much further distant, the light reflected from Jupiter itself added to the illumination. Callisto was much more reflective than the Moon. It dazzled, its light shining in the viewing windows and throwing shadows on the back wall.

The Captain's voice came over the intercom, "Callisto – Orbital insertion confirmed. Ladies and Gentlemen, we've arrived." Turning to her co-pilot, "Please send a full copy of the log back to Control. Confirming orbit and the commencement of surface scanning."

The co-pilot nodded and prepared the transmission. If there was something on Callisto, it might not react well to their arrival. It was important that Ground Control had the most up-to-date information in case something happened.

"All crew, please meet me in the main lounge for a celebratory glass of Champagne."

The ship began a systematic scan of the Callisto surface. Each orbit, the ship adjusted its flight path. Soon all the moon below would be mapped in detail.

...

A new atmosphere of tension filled the ship; nothing had changed, but everything had changed at the same time. Now, all airlocks were kept sealed. Everyone had their suits handy at all times. Dollars had been on a spacewalk with only the Captain. This was very unusual; what he'd been up to was never discussed, and Julian decided Dollars would tell him if and when he could. Julian was reminded of Dollar's words in Earth orbit regarding the possibility of the aliens still being on Callisto and being aggressive. Dollar's response was one word. 'Boom'. Julian imagined a plasma weapon or a torpedo fitted with a tactical nuke sitting on the hull, ready to launch if they were attacked.

This only added to the mystery around Dollars. There was no way the US government would have given NASA a weapon system. How could Dollars have commandeered a weapon and then smuggled it onto the 'Callisto' without the US finding out?

...

The Captain's voice was tight, "Nothing, no energy emissions at all?"

"There's no evidence of anything unusual on the moon; it's completely dead. Our mapping data will keep astronomers back on Earth busy for years. But there was no trace of whatever or whoever had left those footprints." The response was both relieved and disappointed.

"Dollars, what are your feelings?" The Captain asked him in a low, conspiratorial voice.

Dollars thought for a few moments before responding, "I'm not sure what to advise. In a sense, this is worse than finding something. The absence of proof isn't the proof of absence and all that..."

The Captain looked frustrated, "That's the problem; how much longer do we stay up here in orbit?"

Dollars only response was a shrug.

...

Sirens screamed throughout the ship, the Captain had the crew diligently practising safety drills. Bulkheads were seals; instructions were given, the Captain's voice audible over the comms system. They ran through various scenarios, ensuring they were prepared for any situation; they were all on edge; it was the lack of anything certain that made everyone tense. The Captain continued the exercises until they were all exhausted from lack of sleep.

Finally, the Captain couldn't delay it any longer. They needed to descend and examine those enigmatic footprints.

Chapter 19.

The landing craft was exactly the same as the one Julian had practised in. Dollars had changed the plan once they got into orbit and found nothing. Instead of one lander, they would take two. The ship had four in total, so there were spares in an emergency. If required, a droid could even fly them down. But that was a last resort. The droids would be needed to fly the 'Callisto' back to Earth. If the droids were damaged or destroyed, it would be a real problem. After all, they couldn't stay awake for three years.

Julian noted with some concern that, for the first time, he saw Dollars with a weapon. Dollars had decided that as nothing had been detected, there was nothing there. In that case, there was no risk of an attack. Or, they were hiding, so better land in force to prevent an ambush. The two ships would land on the raised plain outside of the crater at about ninety degrees from each other. This would make it harder for the two landers to both be attacked simultaneously once they were on the ground. If something attacked one, the other could take off or come to assist. Both landers carried weapons. Julian hoped they would stay locked away in the storage box. They had enough wars on Earth; they didn't need to travel all the way to Jupiter just to start another.

Neither ship would land in the crater itself. They didn't want to risk disturbing the footprints, which meant a walk. The suits could hold at least fifteen hours of air. Dollars would be able to operate for longer.

Julian had overheard Dollars having some heated discussions with the Captain about what would happen if the aliens were hostile. Dollars had made it clear that if there was a fight, she was to leave him to cover their extraction and make a run for it. She wasn't happy about abandoning him alone on Callisto with no way off. Julian thought it was odd to have an argument about something that might never happen, but that was the military way – always looking on the bright side!

Chapter 20.

Julian bounced along; he'd spent enough time on the Moon not to make a complete fool of himself in the low gravity. But it was fun once you got the hang of it. Each lander had carried four, Julian and Dollars in one, with the Captain and a Med Tech. The other ship had the co-pilot and another Med tech, as well as the ship's astro biologist and an astronomer. Each specialist wanted to get samples or take measurements on the way to the crater, but the Captain had been very clear that they check out the footprints and ensure they were alone before anything else.

The rim of the crater rose up in front of Julian, the ground had been forced up by the impact that had formed the crater.

"All crew, please check in." The Captain's voice was clearer in his headphones than it would have been if she'd been shouting at him across the same distance on the Earth. Each of the eight checked off.

"Everyone stay on the ridge top. I'm going down first." Dollar's tone, not allowing any debate. Julian watched as he started down the slope of the crater side. At some point in the last four billion years, there'd been a partial collapse, and this gave Dollars a shallow slope to descend. No one appeared to attack him, so once he reached the bottom of the crater, he drew his weapon and, taking a covering position, instructed the rest to follow him down. Julian could make out the footprints, but they were about half a kilometre away. As the light caught them, they stood out.

There was a clear trail to follow, but who left them and where they led wasn't as apparent as were the footprints themselves.

"Julian, with me. Let's check out those footprints. The rest of you move forward slowly. Suggest you follow MY footprints." There was a note of humour in Dollar's voice.

Julian walked towards the footprints. He felt as though he was in a cathedral. He didn't even want to put his foot down hard in case they collapsed. The bottom of the crater was a thick layer of dust. The footprints were in the dust rather than the actual surface. Raising his camera up, he began taking photos, just in case he disturbed the very thing he'd come to see.

"There's considerable micro-meteor impacts within the footprints. The edges have begun to crumble away. I'll have to check the number of impacts per square meter, but at a guess, they're very, very old. Not recent. These footprints are ancient, billions of years, not millions." They were truly ancient in a way that was impressive, even to a palaeontologist. His voice was transmitted to all those around him and back up to the ship, to be recorded for transmission to Earth.

"So shall we follow the 'Yellow Brick Road' Doc?" Asked Dollars, he was still standing guard, his gun up and scanning the horizon.

"Yes, they lead towards the crater wall this way." Julian gestured with his head and then realised that no one could see him, so he raised his arm in the direction the footprints led.

It took some time to cover the three kilometres to the edge of the crater. The footprints had just appeared in the dust. There was nothing there now. But perhaps billions of years ago, a ship had landed in this crater, and someone, or something, had gotten out and walked over to the crater wall.

As they got closer, it was clear that they were aiming for a dark patch on the wall. Once it was close, this resolved into a cave entrance. It had been hard to follow the footsteps in places, and at times, it appeared that there were many, not just one. Dollars waited for all of the others to catch up before entering the cave.

"Stay here. If you hear me screaming, it's probably just my mother-in-law in there." Even Julian thought the line was a bit corny. But Dollars was just trying to help everyone relax.

After a few moments of silence, Dollars called the 'all-clear', and they entered the cave. It wasn't just a single chamber but a large complex that extended deep under the plain surrounding the crater.

"No one wanders off." Dollars instructed. No chance, thought Julian. The scientists would want to collect samples. The others were in stunned silence. It was truly breathtaking. It was impossible to tell if the cave system was natural or possibly artificial.

"Hey, I've found something." Someone called over the comms. Based on her accent, it could have been the Brazilian Med Tech.

"Who are you, and where are you?" Dollars sounded a little frustrated.

"Large tunnel on the left, then follow it down. I've left a couple of chem-lights as markers." Was the reply.

Julian could hear Dollars swearing under his breath about people never listening when someone says, 'Don't wander off.' What's the first bloody thing they do!

"Open comms, Dollars. As much as I agree with your sentiments, let's keep it polite." The Captain's voice cut through before Dollars had a chance to say anything really spicy.

Everyone was moving ahead of Dollars, and this annoyed him even more, but it appeared to Julian that if no one had attacked them yet, then maybe they were totally alone. The makers of those footprints being nothing more than an ancient memory.

They moved deeper into the cave complex, following the trail of lights, and then the whole area opened up around them, their helmet lights not even reaching the chamber's roof. Again, Julian had the feeling of being in a cathedral.

Standing in the centre of the vast open space was a cube some three meters on a side. It was of a metallic material and was covered from top to bottom in a sort of hieroglyphics.

This time, it wasn't only Dollars that started muttering expletives under their breath.

Chapter 21.

No one said anything. All Julian could hear from his headphones was the breaths of those around him. The Captain getting her wits back faster than most.

"Air tank check, sound off..." Was her explicit instruction. Each member of the team gave the air they had left in their tanks. No one was in any danger. "Start scanning, passive only. I want a scan of every square inch. If it crumbles because of our presence, I need to have a record."

Julian followed his instructions and began scanning the side in front of him.

"What about the top?" Someone asked.

"I'll jump up and take a look, but only once you're finished scanning. If it disintegrates because of the shock of my landing back down, I'll be in trouble." Dollars said.

Julian had expected a witty remark, but clearly, even Dollars was overwhelmed with what they were looking at. Once the scanning was complete, the Captain authorised Dollars to jump high enough to see the top surface. After Dollars landed back down and the 'Cube' didn't crumble to dust, Julian heard the single collective sigh from all those in the cave.

"The tops blank, as far as I can tell." Confirmed Dollars.

"Please check the surrounding area. we're so focused on this 'Cube' that we might miss something important." The Captain asked.

Each of them stepped very carefully around the cube, looking where they were putting their feet. There appeared to be no evidence of how the cube was brought in here. There were no tracks or other marks to indicate how it was moved into place.

Julian looked at the hieroglyphics and pictograms. Each surface was divided into many small panels. There was a small border around each panel, indicating it might cover a separate subject.

Then he saw it, and his legs felt weak. He dropped to his knees in front of the Cube.

The third panel along had a much larger image than most. An almost exact likeness of two human beings, too tall, but definitely humanoid. Perhaps male and female. He took another scan of it, just in case, and then called the Captain over to have a look.

She just stood next to him. She reached out and took his gloved hand in hers. Was this what the makers of this cube looked like? Next to the human image was a series of smaller panels. One was a map of the solar system, and the planets were all there, but the fourth was highlighted. Mars. The makers of this cube were Martians.

There were more panels. They appeared to convey an account of the history of life on Mars. It followed the development of life on Earth, so it wasn't clear which planet was being referred to. Another engraving might have shown a dying world. That had to be Mars.

Julian drew Abi's attention to the next panel. It was another Solar system map, with an arrow going from the fourth planet to the third. The arrow was marked with something that could have been a DNA double helix.

As their world began dying, the Martians had seeded Earth with their DNA.

The truth was utterly breathtaking – They, the human race, were all Martians!

Those ancient Martians knew their world would soon no longer support life. They must have known the same details about the moon Callisto as did NASA, that its surface was a time capsule. They decided to leave a monument, a tombstone, to their now long-gone civilisation. So that at least something would remain.

Chapter 22.

The crew began the exhausting process of bringing the scanning equipment into the cave; it would be set up inside a large pressure tent. Even the ever-cheerful Dollars was starting to get snappy. It was hard work in the suits. Although it didn't feel like they had the same weight, the equipment definitely had the same mass.

The tent was simply that: a huge tent that was inflated with air, with an airlock for entry. It meant that the astronauts could work without their full suits. There was space in the tent for three or four. It had been a difficult task to seal the base of the tent to the cave floor around the cube. They had a kind of expanding foam, which formed an airtight seal all around the base of the tent. The air pressure in the tent wasn't close to Earth normal; it was even less than suit pressure, but it meant they could work without helmets and gloves for a short period of time.

The air in the tent was impossibly cold, but the large lights provided some heat; each specialist carried out tests, and some samples were taken off the surface to check for biological material, although that was highly unlikely, if it had been in this cave for something like three, or closer to four, billion years.

Each team had a few minutes; two worked, and another had to stand guard, fully suited to assist those without helmets in the event of an emergency. That was probably the least popular job of the whole mission.

Julian and the Captain had been assigned to carry out a fine scan of some areas of abrasion near a central panel. It looked like something had fallen or dripped and slightly abraded the surface. By scanning in a range of frequencies, they hoped that they could make out the image. There also appeared to be a small hole, but whether that was intentional or evidence of damage was unclear.

"Look at this." Julian pointed to the scanner screen, "What does that look like to you?"

The Captain leaned into the screen, and their heads touched. Julian felt that familiar thrill he had any time Abi got close.

"Could it be a DNA double helix, but what's that line? An arrow?" Abi asked.

"It's pointing down towards that hole we thought was damaged." Julian was helpfully pointing to the presumed damage, just in case the Captain wasn't sure which bit he meant.

"But how do those two things match up, a DNA symbol, but how would you provide one in an effective vacuum? What's it for? What happens if you provide a sample? A sample of what?" The Captain asked, she thought she was talking only to Julian, but of course, she was on open comms.

"Blood sample, that would be my guess." It was Sofia; she was still wearing her suit, but she'd heard just fine through the radio. "If that was left by the Martians, and they seeded the Earth with their DNA, then they might want a way of testing if it worked. Maybe it unlocks something? Anyway, your times up, suits on. Let's return to the ship; we can analyse everything and get you two checked over."

The Captain and Julian were reluctant to leave, like over-excited kids, with their new discovery. However, the procedure was clear: they needed to communicate this to NASA, although they were very much on their own. They could not know what would happen if they submitted a blood sample to the cube. Would it reveal some new technologies or release a terrible weapon?

This couldn't be their decision alone.

...

Dollars squinted at the screen, "So you think it takes a blood sample? What is it for? Does it unlock something?"

"We don't know; we're going to need to send an encrypted transmission to Earth using the covert medical channel. Then, it'll take a while for them to consider the problem and send back a reply." The Captain was also trying to see the image around Dollar's big head.

"Maybe it's a bomb." Dollars suggested, "To wipe out any invaders."

"Why bother to seed the Earth with your DNA if you're then going to blow them up as soon as they find your memorial? That doesn't really make a lot of sense." Julian countered.

"Sorry, I'm looking on the bright side again. Maybe just this once, someone isn't trying to kill us." Dollars grinned at them both.

The Captain turned away to arrange the transmission back to NASA with the simple question – 'What do we do?'

...

It took hours for the reply to be received; everyone was on edge, all the crew knew of the discovery. There was no point keeping it a secret on board the ship. If it was a bomb of some sort, it might kill them whether they knew or not, so to involve them seemed only fair. Julian tried to read anything he could find in the ship's library on what Mars might have been like. What insights it might give him into the minds that left that cube wasn't obvious, but he needed to do something. Dollars would check his supply of weapons, and the Captain would pace her ship. Julian could only read. That was his way of taking control in a situation totally out of his control.

The Comms Officer called everyone to the Control room; the Captain beat everyone else there. "There's an encrypted message burst for you. It needed to be unlocked." The Comms Officer moved away from the panel to allow the Captain to enter her biometrics. Isaiah Wilson's face was staring out at them, it must have been dark in Texas as his office was illuminated with those annoying overhead lights that were perfectly designed to cause eye strain.

"Thank you for your data packet; I'm afraid our response isn't going to be very helpful. It would appear unlikely that the Martians would have left a bomb or some other device to destroy anyone that triggers it. I'm sure Dollars will be able to tell you all about the systems he'd use to destroy the ship if he needed to. He's a dangerous guy. Dollars, really miss you. Things are getting a 'bit lively' to use your phrase. Relations with Richmond are tenser than ever. We suspect they've gotten some idea of what's happening at Callisto, but as yet, they've made no overt acts."

Dollars looked almost emotional at the words of his friend, and his left foot clawed the floor a few times at the thought of the Richmond administration.

"It's been decided here that we're going to have to let you sort this; you have a good range of specialists. I'd suggest you get two volunteers to submit the sample, and the rest of you stay in orbit, or, even better, move the ship to the other side of Jupiter. The other alternative is to use a Droid, but there's no way of knowing how the Martian technology might react to the presence of a machine. Sorry to dump this back on you, but that's how it is." Ops Director Isaiah Wilson concluded with a shrug, and the screen went blank.

"Well, that was bloody useless. Thanks, mate." Said Dollars, and several people in the room agreed. "I'd suggest that I take the sample. Captain, you move the ship to Jupiter Orbit, once I've received your transmission, then I'll proceed." Dollars started towards the door as though it were a done deal.

"Thank you, Dollars, but I'm pulling rank. This is not an immediate military threat; therefore, I'm still in control." To Julian, it sounded like she was quoting from an instruction manual that he'd not seen—obviously, something for the senior crew's eyes only.

Dollars stopped mid-step and slowly turned to the Captain. Initially, Julian thought he'd argue. But he just nodded and stood against a wall.

"I'm going to do this; we have no idea what will happen. I won't ask anyone else to do something that I'm not prepared to do myself. If it triggers some sort of communication device, then I'll try and communicate with the Martians; if not, then I'll play it by ear." The Captain explained, the rest of the crew were still speechless after the little exchange with Dollars, but none appeared in a rush to volunteer.

"You shouldn't go alone." Said Dollars quietly, and he glanced briefly at Julian.

"Given the age of the thing, then maybe you should take me along..." Julian ran down as she looked at him, with gratitude and love, but also dismissive of his offer.

Sofia spoke, her voice very calm and professional, as though she were reciting the minutes of a board meeting. "It would make sense to take a male and female; the blood samples should be from them. From a mission point of view, Julian is here for the 'footprints'; he's also the most expendable member of the crew. Sorry, no offence intended, but your role, your expertise is palaeontology. A Med Tech would be a good choice, but could we afford to lose one? It's still a long way home. The other specialists are all going to be needed for the rest of the mission, assuming there is a rest of the mission. Dollar's skills may be needed in an emergency. Captain, if you are going, then the only other male is Dr Julian Richards." Sofia's tone was dead, final, like a judge delivering the sentence of execution.

"You can't argue with Swiss logic, guess you just volunteered." Dollars nodded at Julian, and for a moment, the Captain was going to disagree but smiled and thanked him for his support. After that, everyone else resumed their regular duties, leaving Julian and Abi alone.

"Julian, thank you, are you sure? I don't want you to get hurt." The Captain looked lost for a few moments, like a nervous child.

"I'm not sure I could face the rest of this mission alone."

"Abi, if it's a bomb, then you won't have to, because we'll both be dead!" Julian smiled at her. Somehow, she'd completely missed the obvious point that if it was a bomb and it exploded, they would both die.

"Oh, well, thank you anyway." She looked around the near empty control room, checking that no one could hear them, and said. "This isn't going to happen until tomorrow, so at least we have another night together ..."

Chapter 23.

The Lander glided towards the surface of Callisto. Dollars turned to the Captain and asked, for at least the fifth time, "Are you sure you don't want me to tag along? I'll be good, I promise." He even tried the puppy dog eyes; they were guaranteed. But nothing was working on the Captain, or maybe Dollars knew it was the right call that they were going alone, and so his heart wasn't really in it.

"I didn't say this before, in front of the rest of the crew, but you're the only other person who knows how to work the weapon systems –" The Captain was interrupted by Julian, who squeaked, "Weapons?!" without thinking, then shut up and looked embarrassed, apologising.

"- If this thing on Callisto is dangerous, you are the only person who can use the weapons; I'm not going to leave the ship defenceless and alone. I need you to get my ship and her crew home. Dollars, do we understand each other?" There was now a real edge to her words; their eyes were locked together, and even Julian could feel the tension. They were staring at each other like two arm wrestlers. Seeing who'd crack first, surprisingly, it was Dollars; he just nodded and said nothing more on the subject. Julian had a lot of questions but got the distinct impression that now was not a good time.

A Droid was flying the lander. It was decided that it would be useful to have one to carry the equipment, and the Captain was concerned about risking anyone else on this mission. The rest of the landing was in a strained silence, each lost in their own thoughts.

...

The cave entrance loomed in front of them. Julian had been here several times, but now it looked more menacing somehow, even the first time they'd come here. Then, it had been a mystery. Now, it felt ominous, foreboding.

Dollars was checking everything, twice. The large relay dish provided a link to the ship. A cable ran into the Cave system to ensure they could maintain comms at all times. It would take some time to manoeuvre the ship into a position on the other side of Jupiter. So, Abi and Julian would need extra air and supplies, far more than their suits alone could provide. There were sanitary supplies, air tanks, food and water. It was like a camping trip. For Julian, it was similar to a palaeontology expedition, but he'd never had a Droid to do the heavy lifting; that was what students were for!

The plan was a simple one, but the whole future of the human race could depend on it. Dollars would return to the ship with the Droid; there was no point in it staying. Then, the co-pilot would move the ship into Jupiter orbit, putting the vast gas giant between the vessel and Callisto. Once in position, Dollars would send a transmission to Earth to confirm they were ready to proceed and then to the Captain to advise her that she could insert the blood samples.

What would happen after that remained the great mystery – Death or life, they'd soon find out.

Julian was busy checking over the surface of the cube; he was trying to get as close to the uneven ground as possible. The Hieroglyphics extended all the way to the base; in places, dust and debris were obscuring them. He was using his gloved hand to brush them away. But although breathtakingly interesting, it didn't reveal anything new that might have a bearing on the mission. Mostly, it was details of life on Mars, the evolutionary process, and the technology of those ancient inhabitants of the now red planet. An expert more familiar with those subjects covered might have gleaned more than Julian, all he could do was clean away the debris and scan in the images to send to the ship. Perhaps if any of them survived this, then someone on Earth would look at these pictures and be able to identify them and their meaning.

Abi called Julian from inside the pressure tent, which was an area where they could sleep and rest with much higher air pressure. They had just enough room for their bed and the suits. A tent within a tent, if you will.

"Julian, can you come here, please?" She called again; Julian had been distracted by the images. He got up from the ground and reflexively brushed the dust from his knees. He slipped off his space suit and clambered into the tent. Captain Abi lay naked on the bed, waiting for him. She gestured with her hand for him to join her.

"We've got a few hours before the ship will be in position …" her voice trailed off as she patted the bed next to her.

"I'm guessing the possible end of the world is doing interesting things to your libido?" Julian said, crawling up the bed towards her, almost as if he were a carnivore stalking some prey animal. Abi's only reaction was most un-prey-like. She reached out and grabbed his head, pushing it down between her legs.

...

The radio crackled, and Dollar's voice echoed around the tent. "Captain, this is Dollars. We've achieved orbit around Jupiter. Please update us as to your status?"

Abi turned in surprise at the voice; she glanced at the time displayed on her suit's panel. "They made good time."

"Please come in, Captain. Hey Doc, you are receiving?" Dollar's voice didn't give much away, but there was a touch of concern in his tone.

"This is Captain Thomas receiving. Our status is good. No change. You made good time to Jupiter, we weren't expecting your message just yet. Hope you haven't gotten a speeding ticket." Abi was pleased to hear Dollar's voice, which meant that the first part of the mission had gone okay. Now, it was her turn. There was a slight lag as the radio signal bounced from the dish outside the cave to the orbital satellites around Callisto, then to the relay satellites around Jupiter and then to the ship itself.

"Good, yes, the run to Jupiter was easy, not much traffic-" Dollars was playing along with the Captain's humour, but was interrupted by Maria, the Brazilian Med-Tech.

"Have you been spending time in the pressure tent? You need to take regular breaks; the pressure in the main tent is too low for long-term exposure."

"Yes, I can confirm we've had several breaks in the pressure tent, resting and eating." The Captain replied, a little surprised at the Med-Tech's insistence.

Dollar's response was deadpan, but you could almost hear the grin, "I think someone's jealous of your little honeymoon." There was an expression which the Captain missed but might have been an expletive in Portugues. Dollars could make anyone swear.

"We are in position, Captain; once you're ready to insert the blood samples, please let us know." Dollars was back to business.

"Will do; give us a couple of minutes to fully suit up, and we'll be ready." The Captain confirmed. Turning off the comms, Abi turned to Julian and asked, "So, do I have competition? Is Maria after you too?" Julian looked flustered but managed to say, "Maybe it's you she's after?"

"No, I've seen the way she flirts with you. But you're mine; rank has its privileges. But I'm not the possessive type. Maybe we could both share you. Would you like that?" Abi asked, a curious expression on her face that gave nothing away as to whether it was a question or a test.

Julian just looked awkward. He hadn't even noticed Maria's attentions; this just made Abi laugh. "Poor Maria, you never even noticed her efforts."

Switching the comms back on, "Dollars, this is Captain Thomas. I confirm we're in position to insert the blood samples. We are both fully suited, standby, inserting NOW!"

For a moment, nothing happened. The blood ran into the small slot on the cube, and then the symbol began to glow faintly; the colour was hard to define.

"Somethings happening ..." But the Captain's words were lost in static.

Chapter 24.

Julian stumbled, as did Abi; they both clutched at each other to steady themselves. They'd suddenly got heavy. Callisto's gravity was similar to the Moon's. The ship had reduced its rotations to simulate Callisto's gravity to help the crew acclimatise. The sudden shift had caught them both by surprise.

They were no longer in the tent or even the cave.

The sun shone down on them from an azure sky. There were thin clouds high above. Their helmets limited visibility, but there was no doubt they were not on Callisto anymore.

"Julian, can you hear me? Are you okay?" The Captain asked.

"Yes, Abi, I'm fine; I just feel so heavy. My legs ache, just holding me up. What happened?" Julian sounded slightly out of breath. They'd been operating at Callisto gravity for weeks. The instantaneous transition was hard on their bodies.

"Let me check air pressure; maybe we can remove the suit's helmets." The Captain was checking the sensors on the forearm. The light was amber, not green. But not red, either. "There's enough pressure for us to breathe for a short period. Let me go first."

Abi slipped off her helmet, closely followed by Julian. "Where on Earth are we?" Julian asked. The Captain looked at him and started laughing. He wasn't expecting that reaction.

"Where on Earth ... I've been to Mars on a training mission once; the sun looked about the same: blue sky, air, thin and cold, but breathable. This is Mars. But not our Mars, but as it was billions of years ago. Julian, I think we've just moved through time."

Julian again stumbled, but this time, it was the reality of what they could see around them that had caused his legs to weaken. Both Julian and Abi had suit-mounted cameras. The Captain slipped hers from the fixing and raised it up, turning it around to give a panoramic view. She then brought it up to her face and began talking into it, using it as a log.

"This is Captain Abi Thomas, of the ship Callisto. Having entered some blood samples into a slot on the cube in the cave we've been transported to ancient Mars. We have no way of knowing the exact date, although given air pressure and other indicators, we must be billions of years in the past. If it gets dark while we're here, we'll scan the sky, which will enable a more accurate calculation of the time. Doctor Julian Richards is with me. We are standing in an open area. There's something that looks like grass beneath our feet, but it's darker. Maybe it needs to be that colour to absorb enough sunlight. We are in a shallow depression, so our line of sight is obstructed."

Julian interrupted, "Do you have any idea how we get back? There's no cube or anything at this end."

Abi pointed her camera downwards; there was a metal disc, some three meters in diameter. It was old and corroded; Abi and Julian were standing in the centre. There was a faint glow, the same colour as they'd seen in the Callisto cave, but it was harder to make out in the sunlight. The long grass was overhanging and obscuring the edges.

The Captain, once again, panned the camera around. The dark grass carpeted the ground in every direction, the surrounding ridge limited visibility.

"Stay here; I'm going to walk up to the top of the rise and scan around." The Captain ordered, initially, Julian was going to argue. But they had no idea how this portal worked, if they got off, could they make it return them to the Callisto cave and their own time?

At the top, Abi just froze. Her voice was tight, and she sounded slightly scared. "Julian, you better see this."

Julian ran towards her, his bouncing strides covering the distance between them. His muscles had remembered what they were for, and he covered the gap in moments. Julian stood next to Abi, he reached out and took her free hand. They both just stood and watched the vista in front of them.

On the horizon was a city with its tall spires stretching up too high; they looked too fragile and unsubstantial to remain upright. Under Earth's gravity, they'd have collapsed. Under Mars' lower gravity, they could build things that were an architect's fantasy.

But that wasn't what caught their attention; striding toward them were three figures who were also too tall and slender to be from Earth. Three Martians were approaching.

Julian gave Abi's hand a squeeze, he wasn't sure if they should run, but where to?

The three figures approached and stood staring at the two humans, each group looking intently at the other. Abi, releasing herself from Julian's grip, extended her hand in greeting. The Martians were clearly uncertain what to do with the extended hand, but finally, one of them reached out with their hand, mimicking the Captain's gesture. Abi reached out a little further and gently shook the offered hand.

First contact, as it were. Wow, thought Julian, all concerns about how to get back to Callisto momentarily eclipsed by the reality of what he was witnessing. He just hoped their body cams were recording.

Direct communication was, of course, impossible. Still, with the aid of drawings in a kind of large electric pad the Martians had brought with them, Abi and Julian explained they came from Earth and had been on Callisto when the cube had brought them here. The Martians didn't display emotions like their human counterparts, but from the way the three looked at each other at the news Julian and Abi were from Earth, Julian concluded they were happy that their plan to seed DNA had worked.

Julian smiled to himself, these Martians were his great, great grandfathers. There are a lot of greats on the front, about 100,000,000 of them, to be precise.

The air was thin and cold. Both Julian and the Captain had to seal their helmets from time to time to take in a boost of oxygen. The sun was already close to the horizon, it was clear that the death of Mars was already getting close. How many years had elapsed since the Martians had gone to Callisto to place the cube in the cave wasn't clear. Despite Abi's efforts, that was one thing they had never been able to find out. Although it was at some distance, it was clear that the Martian city was crumbling. Mars was dying, and the Martians were dying along with it, their whole civilisation falling to dust around them. The realisation that the mission to seed their DNA on the Earth had worked appeared to give them some consolation, as did the fact that the humans had travelled to Callisto, found the monument and activated the portal. At least their existence wasn't entirely wasted, something of them remained.

The cube was a monument to their civilisation, and the human race was a monument to them.

Chapter 25.

As the Sun touched the horizon one of the Martians gestured towards the metal disc in a way that was startlingly human.

"Guess it's time for us to leave." Said Julian, his head still spinning.

The Captain appeared reluctant, but as the three figures moved towards the disc themselves, she had little choice. They were about a meter taller, which gave them an intimidating appearance, although nothing had happened to make either human feel unsafe.

Abi and Julian stood in the centre of the disc in the place they'd arrived some hours before. "Dollars is going to be so stressed when we get back; we must have been gone for hours." Julian whispered to the Captain. Abi's only response was a shrug.

The closest Martian touched something, and Mars, the grass, the ancient city and the Martians themselves all vanished, and they were standing in the tent in front of the cube exactly where they'd been standing before they'd left.

"Captain, please confirm last transmission. It was garbled. Did you say you were ready to insert the samples?" Dollar's voice came through their radios.

"Please repeat last. Are you ready to insert samples?"

"Dollars, we've inserted the samples and returned; we'll update you when you arrive. We have got a lot to talk about." The Captain's voice was hushed, almost in awe of what they had just experienced.

"We've come back to the second we left. I'd half expected to see Dollars pacing the tent like an expectant father waiting for us to return, but beyond a moment's static, we might as well have never left. We better check the body cam footage, or everyone's going to think we've made the whole thing up." Julian was beyond awe at what had happened. A few months ago, he'd been unearthing fossil footprints, and now he'd walked on ancient Mars.

If he went there now, would he be able to find a trace of his own ancient footprints – His mind reeled at the thought. Oh yes, they had a lot to tell Dollars and the rest of the crew.

As to what this would all mean for those on Earth, was even more impossible to guess.

Chapter 26.

Isaiah Wilson sat in his office staring at the large cube displayed on the screen, Charity was swearing quietly to herself in a way that would have impressed Dollars. He really missed Dollars. No matter how serious things got, you could always rely on Dollars to say something amusing that would break the tension, and lower the tone.

And things were serious, the US administration had somehow found out that an important discovery had been made on Callisto. Something that would be damaging to them. What they actually knew wasn't clear, but the sudden increase in the anti-NASA rhetoric out of Richmond implied they knew something and feared its impact on their grip on control.

The images had been sent encrypted, along with the medical reports. It had been hoped that they'd just appear as routine medical data. However, no organisation as large as NASA could be entirely 'watertight'. Without Dollars, security just wasn't as good. But he needed to be on this mission.

"How do you think Richmond will react?" Charity asked. "What impact will it have on their power base if it turns out Adam and Eve were Martians?" She gestured to the image of the two humanoids on the side of the Cube.

"For some, it'll not matter. They'll just think it's all fake."

"Along with the Dinosaur bones and climate change," Muttered Charity.

"But for most, it'll destroy their whole worldview. There's going to be huge unrest. Under other circumstances, it would have been good to have taken time to prepare people for the news. But I don't think they'll give us that time. This is 'life-or-death' for the 'Reborn' mob. Enough people will reject them to make their position impossible. If they're lucky, they'll just spend the rest of their lives in prison. They may just get ripped to pieces." Said Isaiah.

That was the real question. How much time would the US administration give them?

The answer was - none.

The speaker on his desk pinged, and his receptionist's voice said, "The head of Security needs to talk to you urgently."

"Please put him through."

"Director Wilson. There's a large mob congregating at the Main Gate." The Head of Security's voice was calm and professional.

"Is it something you can handle? There are always a few." Asked Isaiah.

"There's a lot more of them. Some are armed. They are a lot more aggressive than the usual, 'Anti-science' crew. Hold, somethings happening – Director, they've got a tank…" The Security Head actually sounded shocked, and he was right to be so. An attack on NASA's international status was comparable to attacking another country's embassy. There'd be worldwide condemnation. This only showed how desperate the 'Reborn' people had become.

Isaiah acted quickly, "Get me Comms, urgent."

"Communications Director, what's happening Isaiah?" She sounded frightened.

"I need an urgent high-power transmission to the 'Callisto' from my office. Please arrange it." Isaiah tried to keep the stress and tension out of his voice.

A few moments later, a 'ready' signal appeared on the screen in his office. He was recording a message that would be sent to the 'Callisto'.

He began recounting the events of that morning, concluding with the arrival of the tank. He finished with, "I need you to transmit the full data packet to Earth, wide beam, in the clear. We need as many people to get this as possible. We're being systematically cut off. The US will do anything to stop the information about life's origins from getting out…"

The transmission ended abruptly.

Chapter 27.

The Captain's voice sounded throughout the ship, "All crew to control, urgent, all crew to control room."

The room wasn't designed for all eleven of the crew. Even without the droids, it was crowded.

"There's something we all need to see." The Captain then proceeded to play back the message from Isaiah at Ground Control. The room was in stunned silence. The only sound was the noise of the motors in Dollar's left-clawed foot as it opened and closed. Julian guessed Dollars was fantasising about disembowelling someone.

His friends were in trouble, and he was half a billion miles away. Dollars never walked away from a fight. He looked angry and frustrated. Julian scanned the faces of those in the room. Some were angry and glancing at the Captain as though she was the one driving the tank. Others were crying, fearing for friends and family at the Texas complex.

"The 'Patriarch' has gone too far; the European Federation will never tolerate this ..." The woman's French accent was distinctive. Others nodded, sure there'd be an international outcry. But could it save their friends?

The Captain called the room to order. "I intend to comply with NASA's request and send the transmission. But we have no idea about the consequences. I felt it was only fair to take a vote. I need each of you to confirm your preference for the log." She then activated the ship's log recorder, a light illuminated on the screen to indicate it was recording.

"I, Captain Abi Thomas, confirm the order to send all the data to Earth in an unencrypted transmission."

Each of the other eight women also confirmed, for the log, their agreement. Turning to Dollars, she said, "Dollars?"

"Fuck, Yes. These guys are pissing me right off!" Was his succinct response. Julian imagined that 'pissing-off' Dollars could be very bad for your health.

"Julian?" Abi asked.

"Yes."

Turning to the Comms Officer, the Captain gave the necessary instructions for the transmission to be prepared. The Officer nodded a few moments later to confirm all was ready.

It only remained for her to press the transmit button. Julian reached out his hand to hold hers.

Chapter 28.

Julian and Abi were standing in the ship's control room, her hand hovering over the transmit button. The ship was ready to send the transmission to Earth, including all the photos, video, data, and analysis. The consequences for those in America would be world-shattering. For all of the Earth, it would be a huge cultural shock. Knowing that it will collapse 'America Reborn.' Her government's whole worldview wouldn't, couldn't, survive this news.

By the time they returned to Earth, America and the rest of the globe would be a very different place.

In hushed tones, Abi recited the words from a scripture she'd quoted at Sunday school.

"... The truth will set you free."

The search for that 'truth' had freed Julian and herself from a life of loneliness. Now, it would free her people from tyranny.

She pressed transmit.

....

'To Have And To Hold'
(Extended Edition)

Story No.1 In the 'Misadventures of Mr & Mrs Jenkins, in the 24th Century' Series.

Authors Notes:

It is difficult to remember exactly how this story came about, it was just an amusing idea that developed through a few stages to the story you have here.

'Carry-On' does Star Trek is the only way I can describe it.

Enjoy!

To Have And To Hold (Extended Edition)

Chapter 1.

"Survey Tech Jenkins, your shift is nearly over. Please make your way to the 'Trans-mat-up' location. Survey Tech Jenkins, please confirm." The voice of Control sounded tinny in his ears.

Although most men would have welcomed the good news that his shift was over, his inflexion conveyed his irritation with the interruption to his work. His peevish tone managed to be both dismissive and demonstrated his contempt for the chaps in Control.

"Confirmed, this is SENIOR Planetary Survey Technician Jenkins, making my way to the 'Trans-mat-up' point now. Thank you." He emphasised his rank and somehow managed to make 'Thank You' into an insult.

Senior Technician Jenkins walked across the barren terrain. The sunlight was bright, but the lack of atmosphere meant that there was no light diffusion. Those areas in the shade were utterly black. Those in the light, dazzlingly bright.

He felt uncomfortable in the suit. They never seemed to fit correctly. He needed the bathroom as well. Regardless, he still resented the interruption. He'd made some good progress in understanding this world's geological history. There were even tantalising hints of a long-dead civilisation, but he'd be able to return tomorrow. He wondered what his wife had cooked for dinner, he hoped it wasn't stew again.

"Trans-mat Tech, this is Senior Planetary Survey Technician Jenkins, ready to 'Trans-mat-up." Most men would have just given their surnames, but Mr Jenkins had earned his rank, and no one was going to be left in any doubt regarding his standing on this mission. He was the only Senior Technician, and no one was going to be allowed to forget it.

...

Doctor Singh loved having a window in his office. Since the ship had gone into low orbit, the view was incredible. He felt like he could almost reach out and touch the surface of the desolate world below. It had no atmosphere, which meant you could see every surface feature in exquisite detail. It was harder for the survey team as it meant they'd be working in suits all through their shifts on the surface. However, it made his experience, looking down, 'god-like', all the richer.

His Recept-bot pinged and announced, "Doctor, Mr Jenkins would like to see you urgently. He stated the matter was 'personal'." The software was very good at picking up on the tone, inflexion and pitch of a caller's voice. This was essential for it to function. It needed to be able to detect the pain, physical or emotional, a person was in. So, the actual medical emergencies could be prioritised. It had clearly picked up on Mr Jenkins's difficulty in discussing anything 'biological' as he would call it. The twenty-fourth century had seen incredible advances in medicine. Unfortunately, hypochondria was one condition that hadn't been cured yet, and poor Mr Jenkins was a terminal case.

"Thank you. Please invite him to see me straight away." Doctor Singh acknowledged the message. He knew Mr Jenkins was never late to an appointment. The door opened, and the 'man-in-question' entered the large consultation room. He moved, as did all crew recently returned from a planet's surface, as though he wasn't entirely sure of his footing. It took people a few moments to adjust from 'real' gravity to the pseudo gravity of the ship. The transition could be a little disorientating. Senior Planetary Survey Technician Jenkins, of course, suffered more than most.

He was clearly preoccupied with something. He was wringing his hands together pitifully.

Doctor Singh reached out his hand and shook Mr Jenkins's. It was dripping with sweat, only emphasising Mr Jenkins's agitated state. It was fortunate, thought Doctor Singh, as Mr Jenkins was wringing his hands together so enthusiastically that if they hadn't been so wet, they'd have caught fire with the friction.

"Please, Mr Jenkins, why don't you sit down and tell me how I can help you." Doctor Singh gestured towards the comfortable chairs in front of his desk. They'd been shipped all the way from Earth. It gave his consultation room an air of dignity. It was surprising that given Mr Jenkins's frequent visits to his office, he appeared to be the only crew member who never actually noticed the expensive chair he was sitting in.

Mr Jenkins sat, or rather, perched on the chair. He looked ready to flee the room as though he were trapped in some infernal prison. Still more hand wringing, and then, without making eye contact, he said, his voice forced out as if it was painful to speak.

"Doctor, I knew something was wrong the minute I got off the Trans-mat pad!"

The Doctor's reply was patient, measured, and even a little patronising: " Mr Jenkins, Trans-mat issues are very rare, but they do sometimes happen. Perhaps you could explain why you feel there's a problem." Doctor Singh leaned back in his chair in a pose he hoped would convey maturity and reassurance.

Mr Jenkins was shortish, balding, and slightly pudgy around the middle. He would have been described as being at a 'difficult age' in previous centuries, although such things were no longer relevant in the twenty-fourth. He'd be characterised as an ineffectual ditherer even by his few friends.

"I'd been down on the planet for some time; it was the end of my shift, and anyway, I needed the bathroom … " Mr Jenkins was still lost in his reminiscences, almost as though he were talking to an empty room.

At this point, the doctor interrupted and, in a reassuring voice, said, "The suits are designed to accommodate human waste if the need arises."

Mr Jenkins' somewhat peevish response was, "Yes, I know, but I just don't like the thought of it."

The Doctor's patient nod of understanding was his only response. Through long experience with Mr Jenkins, Doctor Singh came to understand that sometimes you just had to let him explain things his own way. Regardless of how long-winded his approach.

"Well, something felt wrong straight away. Once I got into the bathroom, it was clear, Doctor, I'm deformed!" The words almost exploding out of him.

"OK, why don't you show me the problem?" The Doctor said, giving a 'let's get on with it' gesture. Even his toleration of Mr Jenkins's long-winded explanations had its limits. His fastidiousness and hypochondria made for a challenging mix.

Standing up, the ever-flustered Mr Jenkins lowered his jogging bottoms, the basic ship suit worn by most when off duty. His deformity was evident; a kind of 'elephant in the room' moment passed as the doctor stared at the deformity, then at Mr Jenkins' face, and then back to the deformity.

"Oh," was his only response.

Once again, resuming his professional detachment, he reassured Mr Jenkins that although Trans-mat 'medical complications' were very rare, they did happen sometimes. He'd consult with a colleague, and they'd schedule him a session in the medical Trans-mat. There was no cause for concern, was the clear message.

"But what shall I tell my wife?" was the almost squeaked query. Mr Jenkins looked around the room in fear, as though the Lady herself might appear at any moment, demanding an explanation.

The Doctor leaned back on his chair, steepling his fingers together, in an effort to convey reassurance. However, it wasn't completely clear whether it was Mr Jenkins or himself that he was trying to reassure. The reality was that he'd never seen anything like this. For once, Mr Jenkins's hypochondria had a factual basis to it. As the old cliché had it – 'Even a stuck clock could be right twice a day'.

"If the matter arises before we've scheduled your treatment, I can only suggest you reassure her by sharing the same information I've been telling you. These issues are very rare; however, they do happen, and they are easily rectified. I appreciate that it's distressing, but it's very curable. Please have your wife call me if she's at all concerned."

With that, Mr Jenkins made his befuddled way from the doctor's consultation room to his living quarters.

Chapter 2.

"Darling, why are you so distracted? Isn't the stew any good?" His wife asked in evident frustration, staring at him from the other side of their dining table, almost daring him to criticise her cooking. She'd slaved for at least thirty seconds over the food-prep unit and allowed herself to anticipate the coming exchange. Her fingernails tapping on the tabletop. With fiery red hair and flashing green eyes, Mrs Jenkins lived up to her stereotype. She relished a good argument. But sadly, Mr Jenkins caved in so quickly that she rarely had a chance even to unsheathe her claws. She was tall, slim and vivacious, taller than Mr Jenkins by some centimetres. Why she'd come to the very edge of human-occupied space and married Mr Jenkins, some 15 years her senior, was no one else's damned business!

Mr Jenkins appeared to barely be aware of her, much less the food. As much as she looked forward to the occasional argument, something the ship would be gossiping about for days. She decided this was just too easy and, therefore, not so much fun.

"Was there a problem on the planet? Did your survey go well?" She tried again, but her husband was staring at nothing, spinning his fork distractedly.

"Yes, it was fine; well, there was an, er, problem with the Trans-mat when I came back up to the ship." Mr Jenkins mumbled, struggling to get the words out. He was unable to make eye contact with his wife and stared at the meal in front of him as though surprised to see it there.

Mrs Jenkins was startled to find that she actually cared for the ineffectual little man she'd married. She began to feel a note of apprehension and sat up in her chair, leaning forward towards her husband. She was concerned for his welfare. Maybe not love, but concern.

"A Trans-mat issue … ?" she coaxed.

"There was a problem when I beamed up, a medical incident …" Mr Jenkins was trying to force out the words, his whole body tense. He looked like he was ready to run from the room if she pushed too hard.

Finally, the dam burst and Mr Jenkins started to try and explain, his words tripping over each other in their enthusiasm to get out of his mouth. He began reassuring his wife that he'd been to the doctor and that everything could be put right very promptly with no long-term issues.

With now genuine concern, Mrs Jenkins sat bolt upright in her chair and asked, "Can you show me?"

She was looking at her husband from head to toe, at least all of him that was visible. Nothing appeared to be amiss. She reasoned that if it were really serious, they'd have kept him in the medical unit for observation. So, what could cause her husband such anxiety, but that wasn't of grave concern to the medical team. Doctor Singh was very well respected. The ship was lucky to have a man of his abilities onboard.

He began wringing his hands together in evident agitation. His reply was panicky, terrified—both of the deformity itself and, especially, of her reaction.

"I'm deformed; it's hideous!" He wailed as if in physical pain.

"I'm sure if Doctor Singh let you leave the medical suite, then it can't be all that bad." There was almost a note of desperation in her voice, as though by saying it, she hoped to make it so.

Had they known that at that moment, Doctor Singh was taking part in a series of increasingly alarmed meetings with medical personnel throughout human space, it would have done nothing to boost Mr & Mrs Jenkins's confidence.

Mr Jenkins didn't move. He just sat, twisting in his chair. It reminded Mrs Jenkins of when a small child needed the toilet. She tried not to let the smile show on her face.

Her tone was as reassuring as she could be when she said. "When we got married, we said the vows – 'In sickness and in health', whatever it is, we'll face it together." She was taken aback to realise that she actually meant it.

In a sudden attack of uncharacteristic confidence, Mr Jenkins stood up and lowered his jogging bottoms. He stood there with his eyes firmly shut. His face scrunched as he braced himself for his wife's scream of terror.

However, she didn't scream; her only comment was a mumbled, "It's almost down to your knees!"

Mr Jenkins opened one eye, ready to shut it again at the sight of his wife's terrified expression. The look on her face was dramatic, more one of surprise than terror. If her eyebrows raised any higher, they'd have flown right off her face!

"Does it hurt? Can I touch it?" She asked breathlessly.

Again, Mr Jenkins' response was one of horror: "No, I'm deformed, darling. You can't want to touch it!" His hand started to pull at his few remaining hairs, but as he released his jogging bottoms, they fell to the floor. Giving Mrs Jenkins a clearer view of the issue.

But rather than recoil, she reached her hand out. She initially touched the 'deformity' tentatively, scared to cause Mr Jenkins any discomfort. But as it appeared to cause him no distress, she felt growing confidence.

Mr Jenkins responding in the way any husband would to such caresses from his wife.

"Darling, let's leave the dinner things and go to bed ... ?" His wife whispered, a glint in her eye.

"You can't mean it. I'm hideous, deformed. Look at it! - No, actually, I'd rather you didn't look at it!" Was his somewhat confused reply.

"Darling, it's a wife's duty, 'in sickness and in health', remember…"

Mr and Mrs Jenkins made their way to the bedroom…

Chapter 3.

Mrs Jenkins called the doctor the following morning while her husband was showering. She'd thought for some time about how to approach Doctor Singh. As his screen activated, she could see his consultation room and the large window with the view of the planetary surface.

"Good morning, Mrs Jenkins. I had expected your call." His tone was confident, but Mrs Jenkins picked up on a note of apprehension in his voice.

Doctor Singh fidgeted in his chair and then, after clearing his throat, said. "Please let me reassure you that everything will be ok. I understand that it's distressing, your Husband's medical condition is a little, er, 'dramatic'... But I've consulted with several colleagues and we're confident that we can put everything back as it should be. His condition is unusual and has created a considerable interest in the medical community. I'm hoping to be able to write a paper on the cause and treatment of such a rare medical phenomena--"

Mrs Jenkins reflected that it had given her 'considerable interest' as well, and she wasn't going to allow some 'do-gooder' Doctors to rob her of it.

Before Doctor Singh could finish, Mrs Jenkins interrupted him by saying, "I've talked it through with Mr Jenkins, and we feel it's best not to try and cure 'it'. I'm just too worried something else will go wrong; I just couldn't bear it. Perhaps it would be best to leave things as they are. I'm terribly worried about the possibility of medical complications if you try and correct the problem." She tried to get the right tone in her words, 'concerned, anxious wife', but also, not to be pushed around. The Doctor's response implied she'd got the balance just right.

"Please, Mrs Jenkins, let me assure you that there's minimal risk of any future problems." The Doctor was both relieved and concerned, at the same time. A tricky medical procedure might not be necessary, but a much-needed boost to his professional standing was slipping through his fingers.

"Thank you, Doctor Singh, but it's something a wife has to put up with, you know—'In sickness and in health'. Thank you for your time, goodbye." Mrs Jenkins, struggling to keep the salacious grin from her face, ended the vid-chat with the spaceship's medical team. Mrs Jenkins sat back in her chair, relieved the exchange with Doctor Singh had gone so well. She turned at the sound of the bathroom door opening and heard her husband's bare feet padding across the floor.

"Was that the doctor? Have they scheduled a time for the treatment?" Her husband asked anxiously. He walked naked from the shower, his 'deformity' swinging as he vigorously dried his few remaining hairs. Mrs Jenkins had trouble tearing her eyes away. But she finally managed to look up high enough to establish eye contact with her husband, his nervousness clearly written all over his face.

He was terrible about anything 'biological'. They'd been married for some years, but he still found discussing intimate matters impossible. That, in conjunction with his hypochondria, made their married life difficult at times. He was always convinced there was something terribly wrong with him, but at the same time, he was too embarrassed to tell anyone what it was. At least this time, his problem was evident. It was larger-than-life, you could say.

She took a deep breath and tried to look as serious as she could manage, all things considered.

Still struggling to keep the lascivious grin from her face, Mrs Jenkins's response was of a feigned sober tone. She said, "Yes, unfortunately, it may be some time before they can schedule your treatment."

"Oh no, I'm sorry, darling. Can you endure my deformity for a little longer?" He glanced down in apprehension, his question plaintive, almost desperate for reassurance.

Getting up from her chair, she allowed her dressing gown to fall to the floor.

It was possible that at some point, the medical team would decide they needed to 'fix' her husband's 'Trans-mat medical complication'. But until then, she would take what opportunities presented themselves. She was stuck on a survey ship at the very edge of human-occupied space. She decided she'd grasp any opportunity for happiness with both hands.

And she'd definitely need both hands for this opportunity!

Reaching out, she took hold of her husband by the aforementioned 'opportunity' and led him back into their bedroom with the words, "to have and to hold', darling." ...

....

Terminal Vision

A poignant story, about friendship, love and sacrifice.

Ahnah can 'see' when someone is going to pass away. One day, she knows the whole world is destined to die when every person has the 'aura'. Only one man doesn't; why? Together, can they save the human race? But, what will it cost them?

Authors Notes:

This was a simple concept: a person who knew when someone was going to die, it's a well-used trope, but what I've never seen explored is what would happen if they themselves were going to die.

This story evolved quite quickly. Most stories have a few steps, but this was almost fully formed as I wrote it. I also wanted to introduce the idea that 'fate' could be changed, but at a price.

Terminal Visions.
Chapter 1.

"Here's your coffee, sweetie. Are you sure you wouldn't want a pastry with that? They're freshly made this morning?" The waitress placed the cup in front of Ahnah.

"No, thank you. I'm watching my figure." Ahnah smiled and shook her head in response.

"If you watch it any harder, you'll slip through a crack in the pavement." The Waitress said, grinning, "But it's up to you." She turned and walked away. Her heels were too high and must have been uncomfortable after a day on her feet, but it did give her an elegance as she glided between the tables. Her figure was, well, let's call it voluptuous. Her butt being close to eye level, was hard to miss.

Ahnah, with just her morning coffee and no pastry, looked around at her counterparts at other tables. There were two 'Pilates mums' or maybe 'Yoga bunnies', who could tell, the 'uniform' was the same. They were excitedly speculating about whether another woman at their exercise class was having an affair with the instructor. It was unclear whether this was motivated by moral outrage or jealousy that it wasn't one of them.

The area of tables was still quiet; a few people had come through to collect takeaway drinks, but few had the opportunity to stop and sit. No one else appeared to have the luxury of people-watching, one of Ahnah's favourite pastimes. It was one of the perks of her job for which she was eternally grateful. Being a freelance journalist meant she could work anywhere, and this coffee shop was as good a place as any other.

A couple of men in suits were at another table, trying to fit an implausible number of laptops and phones on the small coffee table. They were asking the waitress for the shop's Wi-Fi code, but given they'd only purchased small cups of coffee, long drunk, the waitress decided that if they were going to take up space, they'd need to order something more.

Initially, Ahnah thought the waitress was overdressing for her role, with high heels, a short, tight skirt, and a low-cut blouse, which she appeared to be in danger of falling out of any time she bent forward. But it was all a way to manipulate her customers, basic psychology. The heels made her taller, and her legs appeared longer, intimidating other women. Her low-cut blouse and dazzling smile helped her to win any disagreement with a male customer and probably got her more tips. The woman's impression of the waitress increased considerably. She wasn't shrink-wrapped mutton pretending to be lamb. She was a 'Freud', wearing a kind of plumage to intimidate and manipulate her customers.

The debate with the two suits ended precisely as you'd imagine – They bought two more coffees, a pastry each and gave her a generous tip.

Out of the corner of her eye, she saw movement...

An old man had walked, maybe stumbled, was a better word, and leaned on the back of an unoccupied chair. Ahnah was about to get up to assist him when she saw it – The light, an aura of colours not seen with worldly eyes.

This could only be sensed by what she thought of as her 'Terminal Vision'. Ahnah sat back down. There was nothing that could be done for the man. Within days, sometimes, but usually minutes to hours, he'd be dead. There was nothing that could be done to prevent it. The Universe had decided he'd die, and the Universe always got its way.

Ahnah watched as the waitress moved towards the man. He began what she could only think of as a slow-motion collapse. His descent accelerating as he approached the ground. He hit with an audible thud. One of the 'Pilates Mums' screamed, the other jumping up and running over to him, the waitress also moving faster, despite the heels.

The two men in suits noticing the waitress's urgent movement before they understood the cause. The two women arrived at about the same time and began desperate attempts to save the man. Ahnah felt guilty for not going to help. But she knew from hard experience that there was nothing that anyone could do.

It had first happened when she was four years old; she'd seen it, and the aura surrounding her grandmother. She knew instinctively what it meant – her beloved grandmother was going to die. She'd screamed and cried, demanded her parents do something, anything, to save her.

The older woman had taken her aside and tried to comfort her, she also could see the aura, she knew what it meant. Ahnah had inherited the ability or maybe the curse. Her grandmother had seen the aura around Ahnah a few days before when she'd had a bad fever and knew that her granddaughter would die. So, she made a deal with the Universe or with God or whoever, to swap her life for her granddaughter's.

Ahnah had made a miraculous recovery, but the next time her grandmother had looked in the mirror she saw the aura glowing around her reflection, brighter than she'd ever seen it before. She knew that the swap had been accepted, that she would die instead of the infant Ahnah. The two stood hugging each other, knowing they shared something almost no one else could even imagine.

...

The ambulance arrived and took away the old man's body. He'd died there on the pavement in front of them all. The two women who had tried so hard stood crying in the mix of emotions that they must be experiencing. Ahnah could do nothing to save the dying, but she could help the living. She walked over and embraced the waitress. Her whole body was wracked with the sobs of the sudden horror, as well as her frustration that she could do so little to have helped. Ahnah held her, whispering soothing words and stroking her hair.

Chapter 2.

A few weeks had gone by since the old man's demise. Ahnah visited the coffee shop most days and she and the waitress had become friends. She'd often sit and chat about life and the antics of the customers.

Looking around one slightly overcast morning. Ahnah could see the usual disparate group at the coffee shop's outside tables. It was a little too breezy for her to stay too long. The waitress had just dropped off a fresh cup of coffee, it sat steaming in the cool air.

After having a sip, she looked around and saw the man watching her from the other side of the road. He was of average height and average appearance, although even at this distance, she could see he was powerfully built. Other than an air of brooding, there was nothing particular about him.

Except his eyes – they burned into her mind, her soul.

She looked away at the sound of a baby cry at another table, and when she looked up again, he was gone.

The place where he'd stood was just an empty hole in the universe.

...

From the kitchen, she could hear the news reporters discussing the latest political nonsense, she was only half listening. She had a cup of tea in her hand as she walked back into the lounge. Glancing at the TV screen, she cried in horror, and her cup of hot tea fell to the floor from numb fingers, splashing her legs with boiling hot water, but she was unaware of anything but the image on the screen.

Everyone on the screen, absolutely everyone, the reporters, the politicians, even the weather girl – had an aura!

Running into the bathroom, she stared at her own reflection, and there it was, fainter than usual, but definitely there.

She had an aura.

How long did any of them have?

...

The next couple of days were a blur, she sat at the coffee shop and watched the people going past. Each with a faint aura, it was fainter than usual, but there was no mistake. The waitress brought her coffee, and she tried to chat, but her heart just wasn't in it. She'd allowed herself to open up to the waitress, to allow herself to get close. As Ahnah watched her bustling between the tables, her aura faint in the daylight, her heart ached at her loss of what might have been. She'd finally allowed someone to get close, and this is how the universe punished her for it.

Then she noticed the same man, his dark, brooding eyes once again burning into her mind.

He didn't have an aura. At first, she hadn't noticed the lack of the field of light around him, but as others moved past him, it was as if he was a black and white image in a colour photo. He stood out starkly against the flow of people around him.

She dropped her cup on the floor and almost ran towards him. She dodged the busy traffic and made it to him. He just stood unemotionally waiting for her, as though he didn't have a care in the world. His expression was unreadable. He looked at her without any outward display of emotion, neither fear nor curiosity.

They stood facing each other, she was breathing hard from the physical and emotional exertion. It was hard to tell if he was even breathing at all. His hair was short-cropped and light brown, his posture giving an indication of physical strength.

"We have a lot to talk about." His tone of voice was so normal and relaxed she wanted to scream. Why didn't he have an aura? What was going to happen? She knew there was nothing to do to prevent it. But she just wanted to know.

He must have senscd her emotional turmoil as he said, "Let's talk, there are some people I'd like you to meet." He had a car nearby, she'd never have gotten into a stranger's vehicle, but she somehow felt like she knew this man. And anyway, they were all going to die soon. Did it matter if she got murdered a few days ahead of schedule?

They drove for hours, stopping occasionally at cafes for a break. She'd grabbed a few things from her flat, and they headed North, heading up to where her ancestors had come from generations before. When you try and drive across it you discover how vast Canada really is. They drove and drove. She'd offered to drive, but he didn't seem even to get tired. As the night started to draw in, they'd been on the road since nine that morning, she wondered what the waitress had thought. They'd become close, she felt guilty for breaking the coffee cup when she fled across the road.

"I need to sleep." These were the first words he'd spoken in hours, she'd dozed off and he'd just had the radio playing music quietly in the background. "I've plenty of money. Do you want a separate room?" He asked without any ulterior motive evident in his tone, but then his voice was so calm and relaxed he might have been an axe murderer for all you could tell.

"No, a twin is fine, I'd prefer to stay close to you. You're the only person I've seen since we left the city that doesn't have an aura. I'd like to keep you close by, at least until we've discussed what the hell is happening."

He just nodded and walked off in the direction of the reception to sign in and pay. Ahnah waited by the car. She looked around; the place was almost deserted, there was peeling paint, the whole thing had an air of 'ramshackle' about it. If the manager had a mother in a rocking chair staring out of a window, she would be out of here, impending death or not. She may not be able to stop the Universe from killing her, but she could at least choose the how. Getting murdered in the shower by some creepy guy with mummy issues wasn't her ideal.

Thinking about it, what was her preferred way to go?

Dying from sexual exhaustion in a room full of sweating, hunky weightlifters seemed like a fun way to go. If you had to go, then you might as well have a smile on your face. Her 'Terminal Vision' gave Ahnah a dark sense of 'gallows humour'. Knowing someone will die and being able to do nothing about it, again, and again, can really mess with your outlook on life.

Although it had given her grandmother a real sense of inner calm, and whatever abilities this guy had, he'd introduced himself as 'Tim', had helped him to be super calm, almost psychopath calm. At this thought, she glanced around nervously at the rundown motel and wondered where the nearest gym was. Maybe she'd just abandon this apocalyptic drive into North Canada and throw herself at the nearest weightlifter and just hope he wasn't gay.

Although knowing her luck, he would be.

Chapter 3.

'Tim', walked over, motel key in hand, and locking the car, they made their way to the suite. The insides were even more unkept than the outside. If you already paid so as to have the key, it didn't matter if the inside was messy. You'd already paid, so it didn't matter to the manager.

"What did the manager look like?" Ahnah asked Tim.

He looked a little startled at the odd question, the first sign of emotion that he'd shown all day. "Exactly as expected, a bit creepy and slimy. If that's the right word. Why? Is this place giving you 'Bates Motel' vibes?"

Ahnah nodded and looked a little embarrassed that he'd picked up on her fears, maybe he shared them. There was a small restaurant next door, this was much better kept and was busy with truckers travelling through.

The waitress took their orders, and they sat in silence for a few moments, Ahnah staring around at the patrons, a few families passing through, a handful of truckers, some obviously friends, bantering back and forth. A couple of cops were sitting at a corner table so they could keep half an eye on the carpark entrance, just looking for anything that didn't quite look right.

Everyone in the restaurant and the few in the carpark all had the aura, glowing faintly. A constant reminder that they were all going to die. Just for a few moments, she'd forget, and then she'd see a little kid with their parents, all surrounded by a shimmering haze, and it would stab her in the heart.

"You okay?" Tim must have seen the pained expression on her face. Initially, she felt like lashing out at him, screaming, 'No, everyone's going to die – even that kid over there!' But there was no point. He knew it as well as she did.

They sat in silence for a few more moments until Ahnah had gotten her emotions back under control, "Yes, it's just a lot to take in, to see everyone with an …" Her voice trailed off as the waitress arrived with their order.

"I think I'll take up smoking again." This time, she tried to put a more humorous spin on things. It wasn't easy, but that's what gallows humour was for. Tim just smiled back at her, "Why not." Was his reply.

They ate in silence for a while, then she asked the burning question, "Why don't you have an aura?"

Tim looked at her calmly, he did everything calmly. He appeared to be gauging how much information she could cope with. Whether they had the time was another matter. Ahnah was almost annoyed that he treated her like a child and was about to tell him so, when he spoke. "You can see the aura, you know what it means, but I guess from the fact that you've become somewhat melancholy, you're not able to manipulate and influence the aura? I'm guessing that, like some, you've inherited the ability, but without any training, you only have your native skill."

Ahnah just nodded in response to his words, she'd inherited the power from her grandmother, but it had skipped her mother. Who else in the family had had the ability and kept it to themselves was unknown.

"In some families, the power is stronger, and so they can train to develop their abilities from a young age, for you seeing people die, knowing they would die and being powerless to do anything about it. That must have been torture."

"My Grandmother appeared to have the ability to swap herself for me. When I was a small child, I had a fever. It must have been bad because I had an aura, at least, that's what I remember her telling me after I recovered. She had somehow swapped, gave her life in exchange for mine. But I've never tried, frankly, I've been too scared even to attempt that." Ahnah felt relieved that she could explain these things to someone who'd actually know how she felt. She'd tried once with a therapist and nearly got herself locked up.

"Yes, some have that ability, even if they are untrained. But with support and time, you can do so much more. I'll teach you to control your aura."

Ahnah stopped eating and stared at him in shock, "You mean I can control if I die or not? How's that even possible? I assumed that because everyone had it, it was going to be like a comet or something, that the whole world would be destroyed."

"Yes and no, it's something to do with quantum probabilities. Possible multi-universes. The exact nature of reality isn't defined yet. We can adjust the probabilities, like manipulating dice. It doesn't take much to change the results. There's a possibility that a comet or meteorite might hit the Earth and kill almost everyone. However, if you've noticed the auras are faint, this means it's still a low probability, not a certainty. Have you seen the difference?"

Ahnah nodded and confirmed that she had seen auras to varying degrees, sometimes intense, as with her Grandmothers and others fainter, such as hers now. In fact, as Tim had been speaking, she'd seen her aura fading even further and mentioned it to him.

"That's because your knowledge is shifting the probabilities just a little. You're obviously a fast learner." Tim was impressed; he, too, had seen her aura fading slightly.

"If we work together, there's many more of us, we're meeting in a remote location, we've another days drive. By grouping together, we hope that we can shove the probabilities enough to save everyone. But honestly, we don't know if it'll work or what it will cost." Tim looked resigned for the first time, his emotionless façade cracking just slightly.

The gloomy silence descended on them like a blanket. They just both sat and ate the rest of their meal without another word. Their sense of morbid dread was so pervasive even the bubbly waitress avoided them.

...

When they'd finished and walked out of the door, the waitress just stood staring out the window after them, wondering what terrible things they must have done or were about to do. She almost thought of talking to the two cops, but what would she say? These two perfectly normal people look like they've just found out their pet dog had died.

The cops would probably lock her up, for her own protection.

Chapter 4.

Back in their suite, Ahnah and Tim went through the motions of preparing for bed, showers and the usual. Each still wrapped in a thick blanket of their own fears.

Tim had suggested that Ahnah shower first, after which she sat on the bed and did her toenails. Why? Who knew, but somehow, the mundanity of the act relaxed her.

The sounds of the shower ceased, and Tim walked from the bathroom with a towel wrapped around his waist. His toned and well-muscled body on show.

"You work out?" Ahnah asked, trying not to make the question too weird.

"Yes, I work as a personal trainer at a gym, I used to lift weights semi-professionally but had trouble with my knees. I have to work out, got an image to maintain. I can't look like Homer Simpson. You can imagine the adverts, keep fit or you'll look like me!"

Ahnah started to laugh at the mental image. She looked at Tim, there were times when the Universe, the fates or, just random chance, gave you an opportunity to live out a fantasy. As her dressing gown dropped to the floor, Ahnah thought that she might as well fulfil one of hers, in whatever time any of them had left.

She reached out her hand, loosened the towel, and let it drop to the floor at Tim's feet.

"Are you sure you want this?" Tim asked quietly, his voice tight and almost desperate, as though he, too, wanted her and a few moments to forget. Ahnah nodded, she also just wanted to forget everything, the tension of the last few days.

They put their arms around each other and started to kiss. At first, it was gentle. But soon, it became more intense, almost violent.

He picked her up and threw her bodily onto the bed. He pinned her down. It was actually painful, with his hands gripping her wrists. Their bodies moved against each other, she repositioned and felt him enter her. She wasn't really ready, still a little dry. But he didn't appear in any mood to slow down.

It was as if all the emotions he'd been suppressing over the day, hell, maybe his whole life, were released in that moment. He clawed at her, his nails digging into her skin, he bit her neck and shoulders. His intensity seemed to infect her, and she fought back, scratching, biting and clawing in her turn. Not trying to push him off, but to get him even further inside her. For their two bodies to merge into one snarling, sweaty, clawing animal.

She knew that she'd be soar in the morning, and probably have an infection from the intensity of the thrusts. But what did that matter? They could all be dead tomorrow, at least she could lose herself in the intensity of the pain and the pleasure of the encounter. She could forget everything else, if only for those few moments.

Chapter 5.

Ahnah looked at her reflection in the mirror, the aura was definitely fading. Maybe she'd just needed a good pounding from a muscley bodybuilder after all. No, that wasn't the reason. She'd started to believe it was possible to alter the will of the Universe, well maybe. But the aura didn't lie, she believed it enough to cause it to fade. This morning, she was paying for the pounding, it had stung like crazy when she'd pee'd. She would be sitting on her sore bits for hours and having to try and find civilised places to 'go' along the way, and all the time, her crotch was burning and itching. Not in an 'I've an itch I need you to scratch' kind of way, just the painful way.

She heard Tim call her name from the carpark; he'd been ready some time ago; he didn't feel like he needed to pee every five minutes, and when he did, it didn't burn. Whoever put a woman's urethra and vagina so close together needed a slap.

"I'm just coming." Ahnah called and walked out into the daylight, she tried not to wince as she walked.

Tim was nearly the same, but she felt his eyes on her more than on the previous day, although you couldn't say he was friendly or conversational. That would have taken a miracle, even she wasn't that good in bed. But he was warmer in his tone and more attentive somehow.

"We've a few more hours to drive, and then we should be there. It's very isolated for obvious reasons." Tim said, without taking his eyes from the road. She'd offered to drive, but he just shook his head. Initially, she'd assumed it was a macho thing, but the new-ish, post-coital Tim explained, "I get really travel sick when I'm not driving; it's just easier if I drive. Please don't think it's just me being macho."

Ahnah twitched at his words, as though he'd read her mind, she made a noncommittal grunt and tried to find a comfortable position to sit. With the car's rhythmic movement and the road's noise, surprisingly, Ahnah fell asleep.

...

She awoke suddenly at the change in road noise, they were pulling onto the gravel driveway of a small diner. It looked ok, but Ahnah immediately had a bad 'vibe' and raised her concerns with Tim.

"I don't like the feel of this place." She just stated it as a basic fact, like, 'I don't like the colour of those curtains.

"Understood, I sense it too, but it's the only place for miles; I need the bathroom and some food."

The mention of the bathroom caused her needs to rush back to the front of her mind. Some cream she'd picked up at a small store had really helped. The older lady behind the counter looked at her, and then glanced at Tim, and said, "Was he worth it? From the looks of him, I say he might well have been?" Ahnah could only blush and mumble her thanks, although she did nod to the woman, who winked back and grinned.

As they walked into the diner, Ahnah's feelings got stronger. It was like a scene from one of those horror films when the hero walks into a place where everyone stops talking and stares coldly at the intruder.

As they selected a table by the window, everyone stopped talking and stared coldly at them.

"Great, this doesn't feel weird at all, why is everyone so hostile? This can't be just normal small-town paranoia." Ahnah asked, trying not to look around too much. Tim was totally unphased.

"Relax, the locals know about the group and think it's a crazy cult and are assuming we're more members. It's a good cover. If people think you're crazy, then no one pays you too much attention. People from our group have been travelling through for a day or two, so they're getting extra twitchy." Tim was so calm and relaxed it was annoying.

"We've another hour or maybe a bit more, the back roads can be unreliable, so let's get some food and move on before they start reaching for their pitchforks!" Tim grinned at Ahnah, but she wasn't smiling. She was almost too nervous to eat. However, that changed when the waitress brought the food to a neighbouring table; it smelled great.

She turned and asked Ahnah and Tim what they wanted, she appeared friendly enough. They both ordered what the other table had just received and waited for their food in near silence. Tim glanced at his phone to check the weather, and Ahnah looked out the window and tried not to look like a crazy cult member.

Even here, everyone still had a faint aura: kids, parents, and the waitress. No one was spared. It was still fainter than normal; but unmistakeable.

...

After eating, they were back on the road, Ahnah felt more relaxed once they'd put the locals some distance behind them. There was nothing on the road, no other vehicles, just trees and fields.

"Bet it gets cold up here in the winter?" Ahnah tried to make conversation, but Tim didn't appear in a mood to talk. The radio was playing quietly away to itself, and the scenery went by, mile after mile.

...

Ahnah woke with a start, she didn't even remember falling asleep. They were approaching a farm, various buildings were spread about, a house, some barns, and a greenhouse formed a very rough circle around a large tree. Under the tree were several cars already parked. Tim manoeuvred his vehicle alongside the others, and they slowly got out, Ahnah certainly was stiff from sitting.

Having extracted their bags from the car's boot, they walked towards the house. No one appeared to be around, it was so quiet, Ahnah was used to the bustle and noise of the city. This was so quiet, that it almost hurt her ears.

"Timmy, it's so good to see you." The silence was shattered by the excited voice of a middle-aged woman who came running out of the barn. Ahnah was relieved that at least someone was pleased to see them. She might be, but the two guys with shotguns that followed at a distance seemed less impressed with their arrival; great!

"You guys must be tired, I'm Emily; this is my family's farm and the base of our little group. You must be Ahnah. It's good to finally meet you, Tim said you were coming. I would say it was a pleasure, but I'd be lying; we don't know whether there's enough of us or what it will cost."

Tim interjected, "We've been on the road a long time, we need a few moments. Emily, please don't overload her just yet. She doesn't know much about her skills, she's powerful, but has no training." Ahnah thought he sounded a bit 'Yoda-ish', but given all that was happening, maybe that was about right.

"I've already set you up a couple of rooms." Emily led the way into the farmhouse.

Ahnah felt very much at home, and her confidence returned, "We'll share a room, thanks." Emily turned and glanced at Tim, who merely shrugged.

"Ok, no problem, we'll give you a few moments to freshen up, and then please come and find me in the kitchen, we've a lot to discuss."

After Tim and Ahnah were alone, Tim turned and asked, "We'll share a room?" he grinned at her, "I'm lucky, I thought I'd spend the 'end-of-the-world' alone."

"I'm too tired for sex, and frankly a bit sore from last time, but I'd love a cuddle." Ahnah had a hopeful expression on her face, would he drop back into the old Tim mode now he was amongst his group? He reached out and led her to the bed. They lay next to each other, and he just held her, she could hear his heart beating, and just for a few moments, she could push the apocalypse into the back of her mind.

...

The kitchen was large and smelled good, there was bread and a selection of food on the table, and people were helping themselves. Ahnah sat down and grabbed a few bits. Emily appeared and sat down opposite her and just watched her for a while. Once Ahnah paused in her consumption, she asked, "So how much has Tim told you, or have you been too busy with other things to spend much time talking?" Emily was smiling, but there was a touch of melancholy to her expression as well.

"I don't really know much, I inherited this, whatever it is, from my Grandmother, she sacrificed herself for me when I was four years old. I didn't know anyone other than us even had this ability, and I've kept it to myself. I confess it's given me a dark outlook on life at times. Seeing someone with an aura and knowing they'll die and being powerless to prevent it. It has messed with my life. I've struggled to get close to anyone, mostly out of a fear that one day I'll see the aura, and it'll break my heart." Ahnah was surprised to find herself opening up to this woman she'd never met before.

"There are plenty like you, the ability skips a few generations, and the person is left struggling to cope, probably some end up in institutions. How much do you know about how your Grandmother sacrificed herself for you?"

Ahnah thought briefly and said, "Tim suggested it had something to do with quantum probabilities."

There was a pause as Emily assessed how fast to go with Ahnah, "Yes, that's the best way of describing it. The brighter the aura, the higher the probability. At the moment, the aura indicates there is a low probability that something will wipe out nearly all human life, I've not met anyone outside of this group that doesn't have at least a slight glow around them. We don't actually know what it is, but our abilities mean that the aura isn't visible around us." Emily paused to sip her tea before continuing.

"That doesn't necessarily mean we can't die as well, it's just how it works. We have the ability to manipulate the dice of probability, to change something from possible to improbable and change the Universe's plan. But it always has a price. That's the point you need to think about. No one can do this unless they are fully committed. Better you leave than try and help if it's not really what you want." Emily again paused to glance at Tim.

"You've got a possibility of happiness now, maybe. I don't know what the story is with you and Tim. Maybe you can have a life together, or maybe it's just a desperate 'end-of-the-world-fuck'. It's nothing to do with me, but if you're not fully committed, it'll not work. But we're already short of volunteers. Several haven't made it yet and we don't know how long we can leave it. If the aura starts to brighten, then the probability is increasing and so the number needed to counter it will increase rapidly. Tim says you're powerful, but untrained.

It's a lot to ask, so please consider carefully if you want to help us."

Ahnah just sat staring at her. Under other circumstances, she'd have called a doctor or something. The woman needed help. But she knew she was right. Her experiences with her Grandmother and later in life, told her that everything Emily had just explained was the reality. She had to make a choice, but if she helped – what would the Universe demand in exchange?

Chapter 6.

The price, that was the question: would Ahnah be willing to sacrifice herself for the whole world, to barter with the Universe? It was too much of an abstract concept. She thought of all the families they'd passed on the way here, the kids with their parents – so much hope for the future. That was easier to imagine, the waitress at the last place they'd stopped; she was nice to them even when everyone else was sharpening their pitchforks. Her friend, the waitress, the woman she chatted with most mornings over coffee. Could she sacrifice herself for her? The answer had to be yes, how many people had died, and she'd just had to watch, like the old man only a few weeks ago. He'd died right in front of her. She'd known it was impossible to help. The waitress ran to help him and gave her all to save him, but it wasn't enough. But now, Ahnah had a chance to save her and the rest of the human race. Would she just sit this one out, or would she do what she'd always felt was a useless gesture – Would she sacrifice herself for a friend?

Emily looked at her questioningly, "I can hear the mental cogs whirring from here, want to talk it through?"

"No, I'll help, I'm ready." She glanced at Tim, maybe they could have a future, but just because they didn't have auras didn't mean they'd be spared. "I've spent my whole adult life wishing I could do something to save someone, now I have the chance. I'm not going to back away from that. I've lived my whole life alone, always fearing that I'd see that damned aura around someone I loved. Not anymore."

"Okay, it's good to have you with us. You sound determined. If we're doing this, it better be soon." Emily replied.

"So, this could be my last meal?" Ahnah had her gallows humour working full power now. She actually felt positive about this, she was finally taking control.

The Universe could go fuck itself!

Emily looked into her eyes, almost as if she could understand what was going on in Ahnah's mind. Perhaps they really did, Tim certainly did appear to have a vague sense of what she was thinking.

"Okay, everyone, half an hour or so, we'll meet in the large barn." Finishing her tea, Emily got up and cleared away the leftovers from lunch.

Tim walked over to her and just stood waiting by her side. They looked into each other's eyes, and Ahnah just nodded. He did know what she was thinking but was gentleman enough to wait for her to indicate her wishes.

Her wish at that moment was another session with her fantasy bodybuilder, at least she wouldn't have to worry about being sore afterwards.

...

The barn was dark and smelled slightly of animals, well it was a farm. There were a couple of lamps, but they didn't reach the edges of the vast space. Emily sat the twenty or so people in a circle, each holding hands with the two neighbouring. Not everyone was here, there were a few with shotguns still patrolling. Ready to deal with any more corporeal threats to the group. Ahnah also noticed that none were young, she might have been the youngest. Tim, again doing his mind-reading trick, said, "There are no kids, it wouldn't be ethical. They're staying in a basement some miles away with family or friends. If it all goes wrong, then maybe they'll survive. We don't know what it is that is going to kill everyone yet. Maybe a comet, perhaps a virus. We've done what we can."

Emily called everyone to silence, and they started to focus, Ahnah was trying to apply the technique Emily had showed her: imagine the person, in this case, the whole planet and push the aura away in your mind, put yourself between the aura and the planet. It was hard to visualise; there appeared to be resistance, like the aura was stuck to the planet. Then, in Ahnah's mind, it finally moved, and she slipped between the Earth, all those families, but especially her friend, the waitress and the aura.

It almost hurt, a physical pain, she heard others gasping around her and knew that others had experienced the same thing.

As the whole barn was illuminated in an aura brighter than she'd ever seen, she knew their sacrifice had been accepted. She clutched at Tim and they just held each other close, knowing it was for the last time. Her final thoughts, even as she clung to Tim, were of her friend, the waitress.

Would she miss her?

Would she even remember her?

Chapter 7.

It had been days before the police found the bodies, a routine delivery of food from a local store that someone had forgotten to cancel had noticed the smell coming from the large barn. The house looked deserted, there was no one around, at least no one alive. It made the national news, another doomsday cult had killed themselves in some bizarre ritual.

But despite extensive investigation, the cause of death was never identified. Those in the barn ranged in age, but none were below thirty, blessedly. It was assumed to be mass suicide, but if that is what it was, there was no poison detected. There were so many questions: Why had they come here? None had any connection with the others in the group. Most had come from this area originally, their DNA had features in common with the indigenous peoples of this area. Many of the locals considered the group to be another mad pseudo-religious cult.

Most of the people in the group had been sitting in a loose circle. However, two identified as a Personal Physical Trainer, Tim Clark, and a Journalist, Ahnah Williams, were clinging to each other as though wanting to be together even at the end.

The deaths were listed as unexplained, the news media moved on as they do to other sensations, scandals and examples of human weakness.

The massive comet that passed by the Earth only weeks later, giving a truly breathtaking light show, served as a distraction from the morbid events in Northern Canada.

But not everyone forgot, some marked the passing of their friends and had a faint inkling of the sacrifice that had been made.

Chapter 8.

The waitress placed the empty cup on the table, it was almost a religious experience, like lighting a candle in church. There was a reserved sign, no one else ever used this table. A single rose sat in a vase in the centre, and every morning, she placed a fresh coffee on 'her' table.

The table where her friend had sat.

As she moved between the tables, she picked up a newspaper someone had left, the headline catching her eye. It had been the subject of many conversations she'd overheard the preceding few days. 'Comet – Near Miss!' Were the words plastered across the front page in large type.

Somehow, deep in her heart, she knew she'd never see her friend again. She had some connection with this comet, how, she couldn't even imagine – but in her heart, she knew the two things were connected.

A stiff breeze knocked over the reserved sign on 'her' table, she moved back and picked it up. The coffee was already cool. Maybe she'd bring a fresh cup.

But just a coffee, not a pastry; after all, her friend had been watching her figure.

....

Ahead In Time

A lost head, an ancient King, a mystery involving the Knights Templar and some split milk.

Authors Notes:

This story was written for a specific purpose but was then redundant. My writer group were concerned they'd be a little short on material for an anthology, so I offered to write two short stories to make up the shortfall. As it was, others contributed, and the stories weren't required.

The basic idea came from a podcast about the Knight Templar; there is a myth that they had a talking bronze head; now, clearly, this couldn't be a living person. But a robot's head could travel into the past, and so there you are.

Ahead In Time
Chapter 1.

Zet stood leaning over his desk. The screen was always angled to give him a headache. It didn't matter how he adjusted it. Just somehow, it was never quite right. The image was always a little blurred, triggering eye strain. This only added to his frustration with the universe in general and those around him specifically.

There was a smell in the air of the laboratory. It was one of those indefinable aromas that indicate something very powerful is working, or something very powerful is about to fail catastrophically. The air almost crackled with the tension. Both from the elaborate apparatus that towered over the two men, and from the men themselves. Their irritation with each other more likely to explode, than the machinery.

Tan Des looked alarmed at the screen. He could see it fine at almost any angle. He knew, as did Zet, that the problem was his eyes, not the screen. But Zet wouldn't accept that he needed treatment. He'd rather complain about the poor quality of the screen than admit that there was anything less than perfect about Zet.

The procedure was simple, but he had a phobia. That was the medical term. It is related to an unreasonable fear of something. In Zet's case, it was anything medical. It was an odd psychological phenomenon that humanity's neurosis had kept pace with its scientific and medical advances. The thirty-first century was a time of incredible achievements, but as with Zet, it was a time of fear to match. The doctors could rebuild Zet's eyes on a quantum level, but his fear of those same doctors stopped him from having the treatment.

A new scientific advance – was always balanced – with a fear of that new science.

But even poor eyesight and a terminal case of Iatrophobia didn't stop Zet from being the best Chrono-Tech in the Sol system. He knew he was the best, and this didn't improve his relationship with his colleagues either.

"I'm worried about the quantum uncertainty factor with this test. The figures are too high." Tan Des looked flustered. He tapped on the screen in the location of the reading, but he only succeeded in distorting the image and making the screen dirty. Another thing that drove Zet to distraction. They'd had this same conversation at least every day this week, and twice today already. The Chrono capacitors were charging, hence the strange smell, and the weird tingle in the skin.

"The field can't escape this room? Check and confirm the field will not go beyond this room's shielding." Zet was adamant, nothing was going to delay this test. His unreasoning fear of doctors was counterbalanced by an almost reckless attitude in all other areas of life.

Before the two men could get into a really good argument, a robot entered the room carrying a tray of tea things. The tray was carefully held in both the robot's hands. It moved with a fluid smoothness that belied its age. The metal teapot was uncovered, and if you looked carefully, you could see a small trail of steam coming out of the spout. There was a ceramic jug with actual milk and a small selection of biscuits. It was a scene that wouldn't have been out of place in an Agatha Christie novel, although it would have been a butler, rather than a robot serving the tea. You could have imagined Miss Marple being 'mother'. The robot turned to face the two men and, with a slight bow, careful not to disturb the tray's content, asked in its archaic voice.

"Would you like some tea, Sirs?"

"Why don't you get rid of that thing? It's got to be two hundred years old." Tan Des said, waving vaguely at the robot, his disgust evident to Zet in both his tone and body language. This only worsened Zet's rapidly deteriorating mood. Tan Des was still new to the Chrono lab's team. He still thought that new things were better. The modern robots could have a holographic overlay, they could have a beautiful naked woman or a mythical creature bring them their tea. But this robot was 'dead'. The externals were just a burnished bronze. It couldn't even change colour.

Zet had worked in Chrono-Tech long enough to know that nothing was ever really new, and he was of an age where things from the past felt reassuring. He liked the robot, as he liked drinking real tea, made from actual plant leaves with female bovine mammary gland excretions! It was an anachronism, but one he relished.

"It's been in my family six hundred years, actually. It is an antique. I like the way it speaks. It's using an old dialect from Northwestern Europe and North America. My family came from there originally." Zet turned to the robot and said, "Please just wait a moment."

The two men then returned to their argument and momentarily forgot about the robot.

"The capacitors are fully charged. It's now or never. They can't stay at full capacity for long." Tan Des said as he looked at the large, spiral structure apprehensively, as though he could see the energy straining to break out.

"What's the quantum reading?" Zet asked. His irritation with his assistant, almost bordering on anger.

"0.93% - Too high. We need to recalibrate." Tan Des kept glancing upwards. Convinced at any moment that a failure would flood the room with plasma, vaporising them both almost instantly. Tan Des feared that if that happened, they'd die, but not fast enough. The machinery hadn't failed in centuries. But he still had this morbid terror of a ball of superheated fire stripping his flesh away in layers. Just as with Zet, Tan Des also had his fears, although he would argue that his were at least based on a real possibility.

"There's not time. Even at that reading, it can't extend outside this room. Set the timer and let's go." Zet led the way out through the large metal door and sealed it behind them.

There were no feelings or sounds, but that was to be expected. Had they been aware of anything, then something would be terribly wrong.

Chapter 2.

As they entered the room, it was obvious something was terribly wrong.

Tea things were scattered across the floor, as well as shattered porcelain and milk. The metal teapot was still intact, but the brown fluid was leaking out rapidly. Zet reached down and stood the pot upright, as if by reflex. The aroma of fresh tea filled the room, now that the sense of a storm waiting to burst forth had dissipated.

"Robot, what's the meaning of this...." His voice ran down as he looked towards where the robot had been standing. It lay face down on the floor, its head sliced clean off at the shoulders. The edge was cut to an atomic level—the metal was shiny and bright in the laboratory lighting. Its various wires and connections cut cleanly through.

"What happened?" Asked Zet, but it was painfully obvious. The Chrono field had sliced through where the robot had been standing. The head had gone somewhere. The system was supposed to send back nothing but empty air. The laboratory's cleaned and filtered air was to be sent back a few thousand years. It would have had no effect, but now that cubic meter of air contained the robot's head.

The seriousness of the contamination of the timeline was hard to overestimate.

"Where, or rather when? ..." Zet Asked, his voice distant.

Tan Des was already checking through the equipment and examining the screens to determine to which exact point in time the head had been sent.

"Around five thousand years ago, but at this precise location. The Chrono field is gravity-fixed, so it would have stayed in the gravity well.

"What was here five thousand years ago? Is there any way of checking for chrono-contamination? We could find ourselves in a lot of trouble." Zet's face was etched with worry and pain at the loss of this family heirloom, as well as the feared investigation into a possible Chrono-Pollution event.

Everyone remembered what had happened when that model Sphinx had been sent back to ancient Egypt. It had created a paradox. Which had caused the other to occur, had the model of the Sphinx encourage the Egyptians to build it. But then, how could there be a model of something that hadn't existed until a model of it had been sent back in time? Kids still learned about that catastrophe at school.

"There's no suggestion of contamination at the point of arrival. There is an odd reference that the computer lists as having a fourteen per cent possible connection, but that is dated three thousand years later." Tan Des looked relieved.

"So, who was here five thousand years ago?" said Zet. "Can we get it back?"

"Yes and no, we can't access it five thousand years ago, as there's nothing to locate. But there is that tentative reference to it in the year one thousand. It's a low-probability reference, only fourteen per cent. But that's better than nothing."

Zet's pain was apparent in his voice. That robot had been part of his family for six centuries. "So, who's got the robot's head?"

"Some people called the C-an-aan-ites." Tan Des struggled to pronounce the word displayed on the screen.

Chapter 3.

King Solomon announced that he would think on the matter and apply his vaunted wisdom to a resolution. Rising from his throne, his regal cloak sweeping through the air with a swishing sound. He stepped behind the curtain and rapidly made his way down the steps, carved, like the whole chamber, into living rock.

"'Ancient One', I have a riddle for you to solve." Solomon's voice was hushed, reverential. "Can you help?"

The room had been here for untold generations. The Canaanites who once lived in this region had consulted with the 'Ancient One.' Relying on its advice on when to plant seeds and on how to improve treatment for diseases. They had carved this underground chamber to house the oracle. They had then even built their royal palaces and temples over the top of this chamber to keep the 'Ancient One' safe and at hand when needed. All it asked was for it to be allowed to feed on sunlight from time to time.

The candles that lit the room caused shadows to dance around the walls, but several were guttering, giving the room an ominous feel. He needed to light another. No one other than the king was ever allowed to enter this room. It was strange to imagine a king lighting a candle, the job of a servant. But no one could know the secret of the 'Ancient One' that lived beneath the throne room of the King of Isreal. There was staining on the walls from a thousand years of smoking torches or candles. The air in the room had an almost greasy feel to it.

The 'Ancient One' was positioned on a plinth in the middle of the room, which had also been carved from the rock itself and was as old as this almost mystical chamber—the 'Ancients One's' bronzed 'skin' radiant in the candlelight.

The lights in its eyes glowed slightly to indicate its willingness to help.

Solomon took a deep breath, he might have been a king, but here in this room, he felt like he was in the presence of a god. Even more than when he visited the temple. At first, words tumbled out of his mouth, but he slowed down and spoke more slowly. "Today, two women came to me with a problem. One of their babies died. But they are each claiming it was the other woman's child that died and that it's their own child that still lives. How can I judge fairly in this case and award the child to the right woman?"

The 'Ancients One's' reply was slower than usual. It clearly needed to feed on sunlight as soon as this session was over.

"You must chop the baby in half. The birth mother would rather lose her child than see it killed. The real mother will suggest you give it to the other woman. She is the true mother."

Solomon was dumbstruck. His voice squeaked and cracked as he asked. "You want me to chop a baby in half!"

"No, you only threaten to." The 'Ancient One's' tone was reassuring. "It will all be fine. Now, please, I need sunlight if I'm to continue to help you."

Solomon picked up the head and slipped up the secret stairs to the roof, where he positioned the 'Ancient One' in the full sun.

"With your help, I am getting a real reputation for wisdom. This Queen is coming to visit because she's so impressed with my great perception.

"What's her name?" Asked the 'Ancient One'.

"Sheba, or rather, she's the Queen of Sheba." Was Solomon's excited reply. "Apparently, she's really gorgeous. I can't wait."

Chapter 4.

The pickaxe hit the hard rock with a chink, and another piece fell away. It was hard and dirty work. The dust was choking, the men's faces were covered. They looked like Arabs, with their heads rapped. Such a reference would have been insulting to the men in the tunnel. They were trying to excavate the old stairs that reportedly led to some secret underground chamber. But if any of it was real was known only to God, and the little creep that had sold them the information. Had he done it for silver, or the fun of sending some of the best warriors in Christendom down a rathole was unknown. But the men had their opinions. If it turned out to be a trick, the creep had better have the fastest ship in the Western world. He'd need it.

The conquest of Jerusalem had gone well, and now they were looking for the throne room of King Solomon, whose famous temple had given the order its name.

The Knights Templar.

Another swing and another. The work continued, each man taking his turn and then back up in to air and sunlight. It was an impossibly slow process. But it was

God's work, and with his strength, they would succeed.

Finally, through all the choking dust, sweat and pain. They reached the bottom of the stairs. Someone had gone to incredible lengths to ensure that what was down here never saw the light of day again. Whether it was the Arabs that had tried to bury something they considered a blasphemy or perhaps it had been buried to prevent them from finding it, didn't matter. They had failed, and soon the Knights would find it, if 'it' existed at all.

The faith of the Templars and God's spirit had carried them through.

There was a large wooden door at the bottom of the stairs. It was solid but incredibly old. With a few swings of an axe, it splintered and broke. Revealing a dark chamber beyond.

It was foolish, but as the two knights approached the entrance, both drew their swords. Perhaps they'd have done better with a Bible or a cross. If an evil spirit lurked here, swords would do no good. But it gave them confidence. With a spluttering torch in one hand and a sword in the other, the two men stepped through into the chamber carved into the living rock itself.

The room was completely empty except for a small pillar, like a very narrow altar. The only thing in the room was a skull. It sat perched on top of the pillar, as though it were a sacrifice to some demon.

They looked about the chamber, but there was definitely nothing in the room, other than the skull. Perhaps it was a relic of some sort, maybe the skull of King Solomon himself. The two men appeared uncertain as to which would pick up the skull. Whoever did would either need to drop their sword or their torch, and neither was keen to be in the dark or unarmed in this forbidden hollow carved into the very Earth.

Finally, one of them summoned up the courage and, reaching out, picked up the skull. It was much heavier than expected, and he needed both hands to lift it. It felt cold, like the metal of a sword. There was no mouldering flesh. The 'skull' was clean and had eyes. It was a true mystery, worthy of the holy lands.

Both men made their way up to the roof, where the Lords and Commanders of their order awaited this mystery. Reaching sunlight, both men were relieved and felt a tightness about their chests ease. It was good to breathe the fresh air again. A large table had been placed on the roof terrace, and the 'Skull', if that was what it was, sat in the middle, with the Knights standing around it in admiration. Its burnished bronze glowing in the afternoon sunlight.

"You found it in the chamber, as we were told?" One of the Lords asked.

"Yes, Commander, it was deep underground and well hidden, but with God's help, we have succeeded."

The men examined the 'Skull', although it was clearly something else entirely. The records that led to this discovery stated that King Solomon himself may have referred to this 'Skull' as the 'Ancient One'. He'd relied on its advice and wisdom. Whatever had given advice to the fabled wisest man would be a divine gift to the Order of the Knights Templar.

...

The 'Ancient One' sat soaking up the sunlight and recharging. It listened to the speech of the men around it. It identified it as a form of Latin, mixed with other languages. Many of which were no longer spoken. As it listened, it began to build up a vocabulary. After some time, it was confident that it could talk and be understood.

Just as the Chrono-Field began to form around it, to drag it, and part of the table, two thousand years through time to the thirty-first century, the 'Ancient One' had time to ask.

"Would you like some tea, Sirs?"

....

An Archaeological Twist

In a remote, desolate landscape, an archaeologist and her team make a sobering discovery ...

Authors Notes:

The idea for this story came from my local graveyard. My usual dog-walking route takes me to my local church. As I walked through the graveyard, it occurred to me that without any context, what would an alien visitor think of the stones sticking up out of the ground in a semi-random pattern? This is the story that resulted ...

An Archaeological Twist

Chapter 1.

The archaeologist's gloved hand brushed away the lichen, small flakes of stone crumbled to nothing, causing her to pause and almost to pull her hand away. The surface was so old, so fragile. But even through the gloves, she could feel the indents in the surface. They must mean something, but what?

Her team were setting up cameras and other scanning equipment around the area, using varying wavelengths, infrared through to the ultraviolet. It was hoped a more discernible image could be persuaded to reveal itself.

The large building located roughly in the centre of the open space was clearly very old, all around it were these upright stones. The indents on the surfaces appeared to convey a message, already, it was clear they were some form of writing, a combination of letters and numbers, the latter *might* be dates.

The ground penetrating radar revealed lower-density material and the possibility of objects some distance down. It appeared that each stone had something buried underneath it. Could they be grave markers?

The computer's software was slowly analysing each image and interpreting the indents in the stones.

The stillness was absolute. There was no sound of technology beyond her small team. There were birds and insects, but no civilisation, only the crumbling skeletal ruins, like the tall building they were set up around.

There was the signal ping from the computer, indicating a result had been achieved, an interpretation?

Hopefully better than the last time.

Chapter 2.

Others of her team made their way to the desks and equipment, some smiled and nodded to her, others were lost in their own thoughts, still affected by the almost physical weight of time that seemed to bear down on them.

Another ping, then another. The software was beginning to create a series of pictures, but even better, there was an initial translation of some of the words, especially the numbers.

One of her younger colleagues gasped, then quickly covered her mouth with her gloved hand. She was clearly overwhelmed by the magnitude of what they were seeing. The numbers were dates, and the best guess was that they indicated the ages of the deceased. The words might be their names or titles. The computer was doing better with the numbers than with the letters or words, but some had the same combination and could have represented a title of some sort.

Another older female raised her hand. The archaeologist nodded in her direction indicating for her to make her comment, "If these are numbers and follow a standard pattern, assuming they counted time from a starting position and moved forward.

Then have you noticed that there are no dates after a certain point?"

The archaeologist was caught out. She hadn't seen that, looking at the computer translations of the dates, it was clear. The other female explained that she'd completed a course in mathematical patterns and statistics before joining the history faculty's archaeological team.

The archaeologist was a little irritated with being shown up in this way, but she maintained her composure and gracefully replied, "That's a good observation. Let us return to our work, and perhaps with time, the computer will be able to analyse more information."

The others nodded, and the archaeologist smiled at her older colleague to acknowledge her contribution.

Resuming her position in front of the stone, she looked at the indentations and considered what this might indicate about what happened to the inhabitants of this place, those who had built this structure. Clearly, they cared for their dead. This place must have taken considerable resources to construct and maintain. The graves had been in use over a long period of time, some stones were far more eroded than others.

And yet, it was suddenly abandoned. The archaeologist couldn't help but wonder what could have led to such a drastic change. Was it a natural disaster, a war, or something else entirely?

Chapter 3

There was no way of knowing the details of those Ancient's calendar, but the erosion of hard stone showed without doubt that a long time had passed since anyone had lived here.

Then nothing, no new graves. What happened? Would they ever know?

...

She removed her suit's exo-glove. She knew it was wrong. She just wanted to feel the stone, to feel the ages of time that had passed.

Momentarily, the sun came out from behind a cloud and shown into her yellow eyes, causing them to sparkle, and her vertical slitted pupils closed down to only a thin line.

With her reptilian green scaled fingers, she caressed the stone, feeling the indentations in the surface and thinking ...

Whatever happened on this world all those years ago, *there was no one left to bury the dead!*

....

Beneath The City Of The Ancients

Two teenagers discover what lies beneath The City Of the Ancients and the horrifying truth that this reveals about their past.

Authors Notes:

This story was written for a specific purpose. I'd been invited to submit a story for an anthology, the organiser was worried they might be a bit short, as some of the usual contributors had been unable to submit anything that year. I offered to write two short stories to help fill the gap. This story and Ahead In Time, were originally developed for that purpose, although they've been edited and reworked a bit since then.

Beneath The City Of The Ancients

Chapter 1.

"Hey, we shouldn't, it's 'bidden!" The boy said, his voice tense. He was looking around as though the original inhabitants of the 'City Of The Ancients' might be watching.

"The word is 'forbidden'. You can't speak properly. You should try reading books. You're forgetting how to speak properly because you don't have any books." The girl's response was snide, dismissive.

"The Priest says that books is *forbidden*." The boy emphasised the last word, making it sound as though it were rude. To many in their little village, books *were* rude, almost blasphemous—another word that he wouldn't have known the meaning of, nor how to spell.

The girl pulled at her newly cut blonde hair; it was shorter than she liked it. Her mother had shown her pictures of beautiful ladies with long hair in some of the old books from before, sometimes arranged in fancy shapes.

She'd asked her mother why couldn't she have hair like that sometimes? Her mother had replied that shorter hair is more practical; we have to work harder than the people from before did, shorter hair is just easier to clean. This was her last chance to explore, as soon, she'd start her 'moon cycles.' Her mum said they used to be called periods, but that is considered a taboo word by the Priest. So, they have to be called 'moon cycles'. Once, women had babies when they were as old as her mother was now. But her mum had explained that now women had babies much younger, so their own mothers were still alive to help.

The possibility of her mother's eventual death made her feel cold inside, and she pushed the thought away.

The morning sun was warm, the birds were busy doing whatever birds did. A slight breeze was disturbing the leaves, and they sounded like the sea. Both children had seen the sea. It was one thing the girl's parents and the Priest agreed on, about the only thing. The children needed to learn how to fish, it was a two-day walk to the sea. They would spend a week with a couple of hunters, learning to fish and hunt.

The girl was perched on a large crumbling stone; she was excited. They had a whole day ahead of them, with no grownups, just her and her cousin, the idiot! As she tended to think of him, but he was a fair hunter, and without him, her parents would have never let her go. She had to tolerate him.

"Hey, try these blackberries, just watch out for the spikes." Her hands were already covered in staining from the juice.

"Be careful, you know I don't like this place, it's spooky. The Priest says the 'City Of The Ancients' is haunted." He was still on edge, but the temptation of the blackberries had won over his fears. One was an abstract concept; the other was a full stomach. His cousin might have thought of him as the 'Idiot', but he wasn't stupid.

"Ouch, that hurt." A thorn scratched the back of his hand, and he grumbled. He tried using one of the words he'd heard his father use when no one else was around. It relieved his fear and the pain of the scratch on the back of his hand.

"You shouldn't use words like that, my mum says it's v-u-l-g-a." She had to sound out the word; it was too unfamiliar. Her father had said something that had made her mum say. 'Not in front of the children!' That was the word her mother had used when she asked her what her father had said. She was sure that the word her cousin had just used was in that category.

The two continued to explore the crumbling stones, avoiding the thickest areas of brambles. They had water, but the ceramic bottles were fragile and easy to break. With a supplemented supply of berries, they were set for a day of exploring. As they moved towards the sunset, some called it West. But the kids just thought of it as Sunset. East was the Sea, South was a large river choked with stones, and North was the country that slowly got colder. There were other people up there, but sometimes they weren't friendly. The bottles had come from the North, but trading was dangerous. Sometimes, they'd rather attack you and steal than trade for something.

"Where are you going?" The Boy asked, his apprehension clear in his voice. They had gone further into the 'City Of The Ancients' than he'd ever gone before. He had his bow on his back and a knife on his belt. But he still felt vulnerable. They were one inexperienced warrior and a little girl. If there were dangerous animals or, worse, people, they were too far from home for help to come.

"Hey, I think we've gone far enough." He tried to sound confident and authoritative. As a warrior or trader would. But his voice squeaked, and it destroyed the impression of confidence he was trying to convey.

"Are you scared? I thought MY cousin was a brave warrior, who'd come along to protect a little girl from the monsters." She emphasised her words to make them sharper than the thorns on the berry bushes. They twisted his guts like a bad piece of food. He looked in pain.

"You're just here to find metal so you can be a grown-up and get a wife. But no one will want you. You're ugly!" The girl's words were aimed at his weakest point. She knew how to hurt him.

He didn't have the words to fight back with, but he did have his strength. Picking up a stone, he threw it at her. She was quick and ducked to avoid the missile. She sneered at him, and her words hurt more than any stone.

"You throw like a girl!"

They had forgotten the stone as they both glared at each other. Each reaching around for a stone while not taking their eyes from the other.

The air was still around them the birds had stopped chirping in response to the thrown stone, so the two were enshrouded in silence. The hollow clang of a stone hitting metal was clearly heard, and the two looked at each other in bemusement. The argument was forgotten in an instant, as is the way with children, and they looked around for the source of the sudden and very unexpected noise.

It took some time and not a few scratches from the brambles, but eventually, they found holes under some large crumbling stones. With only a few patches of light making its way through other cracks and holes, they could see steps leading away into the darkness.

Chapter 2.

The birds, having somehow sensed the danger of flying stones was passed, began singing and chirping to each other. The children followed the cracks and holes in the floor, careful not to fall through themselves. The steps had been a long way down at the point the stone had fallen through. But as they traced out the steps, they slowly got closer to the surface. Finally, they found stone steps leading down into a cave. But not a natural one, but one made by the 'Ancients'.

"We can't. It's dangerous – Bears live in caves." Even he knew his excuse was meaningless. There hadn't been a bear in years. He'd only heard stories of them. One of the older warriors had seen one when he was much younger. They'd come from another 'City Of The Ancients'. Someone else had said they'd heard bears lived in caves. It was a thin excuse, but he wasn't about to reveal his terror to his cousin. She'd tease him about it for Moons!

"Don't affrighted." Even she was nervous, and it made her speak in the common words of the village, she momentarily forgot she was supposed to be the clever one.

The two just stood there staring down into the cave. There were crumbling rocks scattered about, but a path was possible between them. There was no light, not enough to see. Standing in the sunlight outside meant the cave was in total darkness by contrast. In a moment of uncharacteristic vulnerability, the girl reached out and grabbed her cousin's hand.

The two of them stood looking into the cave as if waiting for something, possibly even a bear, to reveal itself. They would need some light. He used a piece of special glass to start a small fire with the sunlight and then began improvising two torches for them to take. He'd momentarily forgotten his fears as he focussed on the activity. Now was the time for him to prove himself. Each boy as he was to become a man, a warrior or a trader. Although, in many cases, it was the same thing. He had to do something to demonstrate his skills to the rest of the village. After which time, he would be allowed to go on hunts or trading missions and even to find a woman of his own. There was no one else to witness his bravery – But this was his test.

It took some time to prepare the torches and the sun had moved noticeably in the sky. It was now passed the highest point.

What some of the older ones called 'noon'. His cousin had found more berries and bird's eggs, which she'd cooked on his fire.

He'd sharpened his knife and strung his bow, twice. He could not put off the test any longer. No one was here. No one would know if he just grabbed his cousin and dragged her back to the village. Maybe her parents would even be pleased he hadn't let her explore the cave of the ancients.

He'd know, and she'd know, of his cowardice – he didn't know the word for what refused to allow him to flee. She could have told him, and probably spelt it for him.

His 'ego' wouldn't let him run back to the village.

"Ready? Those eggs were great. Let's go before the torches burn out." She, too, was scared, but somehow, this adventure, this desire to explore one last time, pushed out the fear. There just wasn't enough room in her thoughts for both the wonders of the 'City Of The Ancients' and the fear of what they might find.

He wanted to lead, to be the great warrior, but his feet had stuck to the ground, like the roots of a large tree. His cousin grabbed his hand as she walked passed, and they took their first tentative steps down into the cave of the ancients.

He had to follow; she almost dragged him off his feet. With his now released hand, he withdrew his knife. He could hold a knife in one hand and the torch in the other. He'd have needed both hands for the bow. He was startled to see a small knife in his cousin's hand. He didn't even know she'd carried one, but of course, everyone carried something when out away from the Village.

The stone steps led down into a large cave. There were pieces of metal scattered about and roots hanging down from the ceiling where they had come through from the ground above. Many small animals lived here; they could hear them scuttling about, with occasional squeaks as the animals reacted to their intrusion into their, previously safe home. It was a good indication that nothing dangerous lived down here. The floor was covered in pieces of stone, which made walking difficult. It would be easy to twist an ankle. The ceiling was partly dirt and partly stone, where chunks had fallen away and shattered on the floor. There was a puddle near one side where rain had collected.

There were a variety of strange smells, dirt, decay and animal spoor. There were some peculiar metal barriers blocking the cave, what purpose they served was impossible to know. Metal of any sort was valuable. They could bring some back as proof of his bravery and then sell it. He might be able to build a house with the money. The Blacksmith could make many knives and tools with this.

"Don't scratch yourself on the metal, it's sharper than berry spikes. My mum says you can get a sickness if you cut yourself on dirty metal." The Girl whispered, she didn't know why, but this place was like a grave. She just hoped it wouldn't be hers. Above the ground, she had been teasing her cousin for his fear. But now she was in the 'Grave of the Ancients' she also had felt the squeeze of fear around her heart.

After the metal barrier, they had seen something that was impossible. It explained what had made the clanging noise when the stone had fallen through. But it was impossible. There were steps made from stone, and some from wood.

But no one had ever spoken of steps made from metal, stairs that trailed away into the darkness. A darkness that swallowed all light. To her, it felt more and more like a grave.

But the grave of what?

Chapter 3.

They could never take this metal back for the Blacksmith. There appeared to be no way of lifting it. She stepped out and tentatively put one foot on the first metal step. It held her weight. There was rust on some surfaces, but the metal appeared much better preserved down here, away from the rain and cold.

Each step they took sounded hollow in the silence; there were fewer creatures down here. There was no natural light, and no rain could get through all the rock above, so there was less to support the various creatures that had made the 'Cave of the Ancients' as they had come to refer to it, a home.

The light from their torches flickered and writhed, like a living creature; sometimes, there were gusts of air coming up the tunnel, bringing strange and unpleasant smells, of rot and death. When the breeze blew, their torches flared, and they could see, but once the wind died down, the light reduced, and they were in near total darkness.

"What if the torches run out before we get to the bottom? We'll never find our way out?" The girl's voice sounded scared and small; she knew how to talk when on a hunt, but whether they were the hunter or the hunted, wasn't clear. She feared the latter.

"They should last a little longer, I've made these torches before for night walking." His reply had a tone of confidence, but was he trying to reassure her or himself?

The girl looked back up the tunnel and was surprised to see how far they'd come. But she was reassured that there was a glimmer of daylight, which was still visible. Even if the torches died, they should still be able to find their way back up to the entrance.

"I can still see light above, so we should be okay if we have to go back up in the dark." Her voice held more reassurance than before, the knowledge that they could flee helped steady her nerves. However, she gripped her knife a little tighter as they stepped out into another 'Cave'.

This lacked the roots and animal spoor evident in its counterpart above. It was hard to make out, but there was lots of rubbish across the floor, old rags, and small metal bottles almost rusted to nothing.

"Be careful, these metal bottles are sharp." Was her warning to her male counterpart. "What's all these rags?" She asked, bending down. She picked some up and screamed as several bones clattered to the floor.

She'd experienced death, she could skin a dead animal for dinner, with her mother's oversight. She'd seen dead people, either old age, sickness or sometimes even because of violence. But she'd always known what to expect. In this 'Grave of the Ancients' to find mouldering bones scattered across the floor, so unexpectedly, had been too much.

"It's oo-k-ay." The boy said, spinning around, his knife out, ready for an attack from an animal or man. But the bones that rattled to the floor weren't dangerous. They couldn't hurt anyone, 'unless you tripped over them', his mind came up with the phrase – It was the thing a hunter would have said to reassure a child on his first trip outside the Village. For a few moments, he felt his transition from child to man, not in his body, but in his soul. Although had you asked, he'd have replied, 'So-uel-ll'?

They both held their torches closer to the floor. The stone was covered in piles of rags, each with bones.

"Do you think these are the bones of the 'Ancients'? This really is their grave?" She asked the questions that were uppermost in her mind, but it was well beyond her cousin's ability even to understand the questions, far less answer them.

This cave looked even bigger than the one above, although that could have been a trick of the light, with only the illumination of their torches. The cave extended into darkness in all directions.

On one side, there was an edge, crumbling in places. She slowly crept towards it, like it was a small animal she was hunting. The stone floor was cracked, but some of the stones had different coloured paint on them. This floor was better preserved than its duplicate above. As she looked down from the edge, she could see it fell away about half the height of a fully grown warrior.

"Look at all this metal!" her fears, and concern for violating the grave of the 'Ancients' were forgotten in the thought of all the riches that they could have, if they could get this metal back up to the Blacksmith.

Her cousin stepped over to her, walking carefully to avoid the rags and bones, as he would avoid sticks on the ground when hunting. A stick snapping would reveal his presence to the prey and mean a hungry family. It was now ingrained into him; he did it without thinking.

"Wow, the metal is very good, not bent or rustish." He, too, was thinking of the blessing this metal would bring to him and the Village. His thoughts lingered on the possibility that he could take a wife. It was a subject that had become of increasing interest to him lately for reasons he didn't quite understand.

The metal ran very straight and disappeared in both directions into the darkness. Why was all this metal here? What had the 'Ancients' used it for? Where did it go? These were questions that hovered in the back of his mind. But they were even less understood than the cave, which was seen only in the dim light of their torches.

They both stayed close together. They needed the light from both torches to see around them. They followed around the edges of the cave. There were paintings on the walls.

"Look at this." The girl whispered, holding her torch higher to illuminate a picture that was taller than her.

"What is it ... ?" He asked, his voice trailing off.

"It must be the 'City of the Ancients', when it was new."

The mural was old and stained. It was like the large glass picture in the window of the church. But this was on the stone of the wall. It showed a very large village, with buildings with many windows. Some appeared much higher than the church steeple in their village.

"Is it on fire?" He asked. They both knew about wildfires, in the summer, they had seen several at a long distance, the smoke of a big one could be seen a day's walk.

The fire and smoke towered over even the tallest building in the 'City of the Ancients'; it was shaped like a mushroom - but was full of flame and smoke. It looked hotter than any fire the Blacksmith had. As they stood staring at the mural, they both reached out and held hands.

This was indeed the 'Grave of the Ancients', at least of those that survived the fire.

....

The Words Of The Sole

In a post-apocalyptic Britain, you'll never guess what's replaced the Lord's Prayer.

Authors Notes:

This story is something that those more familiar with British culture may understand. How this idea came about is difficult to explain, at least without giving away the story. Thousands of people listen to it every day, and to many, it's poetry.

'The Words Of The Sole.'

"Amen." The congregation uttered the word in a melodious tone, the sound filling the old church. The word echoed back from the walls and vaulted ceiling. The Morning sun shining in through the stained-glass window, illuminating the pews in a dazzling range of colours. Dust motes danced in the beams of multi-coloured light.

As the Farmer made his way out of the church, he shook the Vicar's hand and thanked him for the fine service. His hand was calloused from hard work, but the Priest's were little different; the Farmer knew he also worked hard in his garden, offering his surplus to those in need in the village. It was probably wrong to think such a thing, but most in the village preferred the new priest. The Old Father had been a bit too fond of the wine and sometimes fell asleep during a service; the Farmer had done that too, after a long night's work.

But not while he was actually giving the service!

"You read the Words beautifully this morning and thank you for having the service so early. We are very busy with the harvest."

The Vicar smiled and leaned in close, "I imagine the best bit is that it was short."

The Farmer looked a little guilty, he'd been thinking exactly that, "Well, we are busy with the harvest; it's been a good year, and while the weather holds, we need to get the crops into storage." The Farmer liked the Priest, but it was important not to show a lack of faith or disrespect for the Words. Reflecting on the Words, a memory sprang unbidden in the Farmer's mind.

"When I was a child, I travelled to a Suffolk port with my father, and we met a man who claimed to be a 'German'. I'm not sure if it's the same one mentioned in the Words. He was very old and sometimes got confused. He spoke about boats that crossed the sea to other lands and brought back many things for sale. That was before the 'Fire-in-the-sky'." The farmer's eyes had lost focus as he recalled the events of so many years before. His father had been dead many winters already.

"Did he try and bite you?" Asked the Priest with a grin.

The Farmer jumped at the Priest's unexpected question. "No, Vicar, but he spoke with a strange accent, not like the Wet Country people or the Northerners. But with sharp words, it's hard to explain." The

Farmer was enjoying this exchange with the Priest but knew that others were waiting to leave the church; he was blocking the door.

Then the Priest said something surprising. "When I was younger, I heard stories of boats that could sail amongst the clouds like birds and could take people to many exotic places." The Farmer was intrigued by his words, there were stories for children of such things, but no one really believed them.

The Vicar, noticing the queue at the church's door for the first time, smiled at the Farmer and wished him well, with the parting words, "All we can do is keep good visibility and care for our soles. Take care, and good luck with the harvest. With God's blessing, the weather will hold."

...

The Farmer walked along the road, enjoying the early morning sun. He heard, at a distance now, the church bells sounding eight. It was early still, they'd get in a good harvest this year. Some people said that once the church clock sounded the bell by itself, but something had broken many winters ago, and so it was for the Old Lady and her apprentice to ring the number of hours showing on the clock. Then everyone around would know the hour and could plan their day's events. In the back of his mind was a small fear that one day, the clock itself might break, and no one would know how to fix it. When that happened, well, he wasn't really sure what would happen, but he had a cold feeling in his chest, like fingers of ice squeezing his heart.

To boost his mood and clear away the fingers of ice, he started to whistle and recite the Words out loud.

Fortys, Gromarty, Forf

Souf or soufeast 3 to 5. Slight or moderate. Mainly fair. Moderate or good

Tyne, Dogger, Fisher, German Bite, Humber, Thames

Variable, mainly souf or soufeast, 2 to 4. Smooth or slight. Fair. Moderate or good

The Farmer looks out at the fields ready to be harvested, the wheat moving slowly back and forth in the breeze. It sounded like the sea, on those rare trips he'd made to Suffolk. He wonders aloud, "Was there a greater meaning behind the words?" They clearly held real power and brought the communities together. But what did it all mean? Was it a lack of faith to even ask such a question? The Vicar had talked of the boats that floated amongst the clouds, the ones before the 'Fire-in-the-sky'. Clearly, the priest didn't have a lack of faith. Perhaps he'd arrange an appointment with him, after the harvest; maybe they could talk of such things over a few glasses of the Old Father's famous wine.

He recalled his meeting with Mr Mackenzie, who lived up at the Big House and was experimenting with something he called 'electricity'. Mr Mackenzie had explained they had it before the 'Fire'. It could do many things: create light brighter than a candle and make things move. To the Farmer, such things had a tinge of the 'magic' about them. Was it more than just a child's bedtime story?

Mr Mackenzie described it as being like tame lightning, but even a tame dog could bite you. Would this electricity bite?

This train of thought took him full circle, and once again, he thought of the 'Words'.

Who really were the Germans, and did they really bite?

....

I'm An Angel, Not An Astrophysicist!

Heaven's three most dysfunctional angels in their first assignment. An impossible job ticket from HIM, and a book about black holes. What could possibly go wrong?

Authors Notes:

It's not easy to explain where this idea came from; when you read the story, you'll understand why. Taking a Biblical account, something most people probably don't believe happened and then find a way it could have happened within the rules of physics and then have three dysfunctional characters carry out the assignment. Well, I can't explain it, I guess there's just a lot going on in my subconscious!

I'm An Angel, Not An Astrophysicist!

"He asked for what?" Freebius said in shock, "How are we supposed to do that?"

Deamanus made a vague hand gesture, and a scroll appeared with a fanfare of celestial music. "Sorry, I can't turn off that annoying notification tone. Here, read it for yourself. It's a job ticket, like any other. But this one is signed by HIM, HIMSELF." Deamanus looked around nervously as though the HIM might appear at any moment in response to this lack of reverential respect.

"But how are we supposed to make the sun stand still?" Freebius asked.

"I'm an angel, not an astrophysicist. How do you expect me to know? Anyway, who asked HIM for this? It's an odd request. Have they found that the universe is running too fast again and need a reset?" Deamanus looked at Freebius with his best – 'Shit happens, but why always to me?' look.

Freebius gave a shrug, "It's got something to do with that lot down there." He gestured in the direction of the Earth and, using pinch zoom, brought a battlefield into sharp focus. "There's one lot of guys with pointy sticks trying to kill another bunch of guys with pointy sticks. One of them asked HIM to make the sun stand still – and here we are."

"It's only over there, can't we just hold it in place until they've finished killing each other?" asked Deamanus with a sly grin.

Freebius looked incredulous, "You know the Earth goes around the Sun, not the other way around. We'd have to stop the Earth spinning. The Suns a huge ball of plasma at millions of degrees, not a candle on wheels, moving across the sky!"

"I'm an angel, not an..."

"You should have that made into a T-shirt!" Was Freebius's caustic response.

"So why are one bunch of bipedal mammals trying to kill the other bunch of bipedal mammals using those pointy sticks?" asked Deamanus.

"Shhh!" Said Freebius, "They don't know they're evolved from other mammals yet. They won't work that out for another few thousand years. They are primates, to be specific. Anyway, those pointy sticks are called swords."

"S-o-r-d-s." Said Deamanus, "I assume the W is silent?" The word was unfamiliar in his mouth, but he liked the taste and the thought of all the trouble that could be caused with one. As he contemplated this, there was a strong smell of sulphur in the air.

"There's an interesting story about swords. In around five hundred years, a King, the smartest man who ever lived, apparently, will threaten to cut a baby in half with a sword." Explained Freebius.

"He's considered the 'smartest man' because he threatened to cut a baby in half, I know the things are noisy, but that's a bit extreme." Deamanus was sceptical. But then he started to think about women and what they had to do to get babies, and the smell of sulphur returned. Two small horns momentarily grew out of the top of Deamanus's head, only to fade away a moment later.

Tristus appeared with a popping sound and a slight whoosh. His entrance was accompanied by a ping as though invisible elevator doors had just opened and then closed. He walked over to join the other two, who were still staring down at the battle below. The sounds of battle, the screams of men fighting and dying, could be heard faintly in the quiet room.

There was a general exchange of heavenly greetings, and then Freebius asked, gesturing to the thing Tristus held in his hand, "What's that?"

"A book." He replied, his mind focussed on the little people running about below, as though pieces on a board game. To them, it was little more than that, but to the men dying, it was very, brutally real.

"Yes, I know, but which book? They haven't even invented books in this timeline, you drop that down there, and you could create a whole new universe." Freebius's tone was curt.

"They couldn't read it, it's in English. They don't speak that down there." Tristus's reply was ridiculing.

"We're angels, not four-year-olds." Said Deamanus, trying to be the voice of reason, which was very much out of character.

"Management sent me down here to see if you needed some help." Tristus tried using a less confrontational tone but failed. "It's 'A Brief History Of Time', from around two thousand AD. It's very interesting. It's got stuff about black holes, fascinating. So, how's it going with making the sun stand still?"

"Not so good. We have no idea how to stop the Earth from spinning without breaking half the laws of physics. We could just stop the Earth, but the inertia would kill all life, which I assume isn't a desired outcome. Or is HE fed up with them again and looking for an excuse?" Freebius was almost hopeful that they might have finally found a solution.

"No, killing everyone isn't the preferred outcome." Tristus reassured. "Well, this book has a lot to say about black holes, I just wondered if there's something in this book that could help."

"I made a black hole once, there's one in the centre of the galaxy, it's not very big. But I was proud of it." Interrupted Deamanus, boasting.

"I thought you didn't know anything about astrophysics?" Said Freebius in evident confusion. "You pride yourself on your ignorance."

Deamanus looked hurt, "I didn't say I knew anything about black holes, only that I made one once, making something doesn't require any knowledge. It's just like making a cake, you just follow the recipe. Take a certain amount of matter, squeeze until it collapses and the escape velocity exceeds the speed of light."

"So, you do know about them?" Said Tristus.

"No, I just followed the instructions!" Deamanus appeared offended that it had been suggested that he understood anything, he took pride in his ignorance, and no one was going to take that away from him.

What Deamanus did want to know more about was women, he wanted to know them 'Biblically' as it were.

"I had cake once, oh, around four hundred years or so ago. It was wonderful." Tristus's eyes lost focus as he recalled the taste and texture. "We went to visit this patriarch, can't remember his name. Anyway, when we were there, his wife made us some cakes, which tasted great. Sorry, you missed them."

"Wife, would that be a woman, that a man sleeps with every night, I mean gets into bed with, possibly naked?" Deamanus was positively drooling, not at the thought of cake, but at the possibility of a naked woman! As he did so, there was another strong smell of sulphur and the faint sound of a tail swishing through the air.

"Deamanus, enough of that! There's been too much trouble with angels and women. You can't tell me you've already forgotten about Noah and the flood?" Freebius was incensed.

Deamanus looked demonically guilty for a few moments, but eventually, the tail and the sulphurous smell both faded away. The three returned to watching the little characters running, fighting and dying below them. The sun was hanging in the sky as though it were mocking all three heavenly entities because of their inability to resolve the problem.

Finally, Freebius said, "So, how do you think we can use black holes to move the Earth or the Sun?"

Tristus looked slightly startled to have the question presented to him, as though he might possibly know the answer. "I'm not sure, it just seemed to me that we might be able to use some of the ideas in this book." He gestured vaguely towards the book he still had in his hand. As if wishing to be distanced from his association with it, he released it, and it floated in mid-air as though resting on an invisible table.

"Could we use gravity to slow down the Sun as it goes around the Earth?" Freebius then realised that he'd just made the same mistake, he had criticised Deamanus for making. But much to his relief, the other two appeared too distracted to notice.

"Maybe slow down the Earth, reduce the spin speed, then increase it again afterwards?" Tristus suggested. Then, he answered his own question, "It's the inertia problem again. It would take ages to do it slowly enough, these people would all be dead of old age."

"Maybe that's the answer, we just take so long that the primate that asked HIM for this favour has died of old age." Freebius looked relieved to have finally found a loophole. It wasn't solving the actual problem, but it was a good way of avoiding the consequences of disappointing HIM.

Tristus then asked, "What's old age?"

Deamanus looked at them both, he prided himself on his ignorance, or at least the appearance of it. But these two must have been the daftest in the whole of Heaven, and that was saying something. "You know, Adam and Eve, the apple, garden of Eden." But at the thought of a Naked Eve, there was another puff of sulphur, and a very unangelic bulge appeared in Deamanus's celestial tunic, just below his belt buckle!

The other two tried not to notice.

"So, gravity, black holes, job tickets from HIM!" Freebius said, trying to get Deamanus's mind back to the present and off the subject of a wench with an apple fixation. Not to mention her worrying habit of talking to strange snakes. At this thought he had the mental image of Deamanus using a part of his anatomy as a one-eyed snake to try and seduce Eve. Freebius shook his head violently to clear away the horrifying vision.

"Why are they called 'black'?" Deamanus asked, bringing Freebius's mind back to the scene in front of them with a jolt.

"Gravity, according to the guy that wrote this book, it's because the escape velocity is higher than the speed of light. Therefore, not even light can escape their gravity. Hence black." Tristus explained, feeling very superior.

"So, gravity can affect light, change it's direction?" Deamanus asked, with his best 'oblivious' expression on his face, like he was a woman asking a man to explain to her all about something she was already fully cognizant of.

"That's it! We position a black hole near the Sun and make the Earth appear to be in a different place." Freebius looked terribly pleased with himself for solving this riddle worthy of any Sphinx.

"Maybe do it the other way around?" Deamanus suggested helpfully, something also very much out of character.

"But how do we create a black hole? Deamanus, you said you knew how to do it. Could you give it a try?" Freebius asked, almost pleading.

"It'll mean manipulating four-dimensional physics." Deamanus's façade of ignorance slipped for a moment in his enthusiasm to demonstrate his skills.

The other two angels just stood staring, mouths agape. Deamanus began moving his hands through the air, twisting and pulling, squeezing in a way that would have appeared obscene to a more worldly observer. A small point appeared in front of him, like a whirlpool, but only of air. As it grew, a halo appeared around it, and then even light began to swirl at increasing speed. A multicoloured spinning point floated in mid-air in the celestial room where they were working.

Deamanus held it in the palm of his hand and then, with a gesture, sent it floating off over the battlefield below. It hovered in place, and as the three celestial beings watched, the already darkening battlefield was re-illuminated by the light bent around the black hole's gravity.

Down below, one group were chasing another group, the pursuers waving their pointy sticks menacingly. They cheered as the battlefield illuminated, enabling them to find and kill their fleeing enemies.

"Great, I'll mark that job as complete and file it." Said Freebius, feeling relieved. He placed the job ticket in a slit, and there was a heavenly chime, and the sheet was whipped inside.

Tristus, still carrying the book, and Freebius headed for the door. "Deamanus, you coming? We deserve an ambrosia after that?"

"No, not yet, I'll catch you up. I just wanted to watch how the battle goes, and then I'll dismantle the black hole." He said, still staring down slyly at the battlefield.

...

"One day, I'll rule this place, and then I can have all the women I want." He said to the empty room. This time, the smell of sulphur was overwhelming, the whole room filling with a positively demonic light. The horns and tail both appeared simultaneously and stayed for more than just a brief moment.

"Oh yes. One day ..."

....

'Never Mess With The Cleaner'

Alien first contact, an unlikely hero.

How a vacuum cleaner saved the world.

Authors Notes:

This is one of the first stories I ever wrote; it's rough and mostly unedited. I included it here for nostalgic reasons. Hopefully, at some point, I'm going to rework it and expand it. I think the idea, that of a first contact, but by an unlikely character, is worth exploring further. So, look out for a new version of this story, although it might be some time.

Chapter 1 – Anubis?

Even with his headphones on, he was aware of the thud; he felt it through the floor as much as heard it. It sounded a lot like the front door slamming. But he was sure he had locked it. He had a system; he would come in, unlock the front door, deactivate the alarm, and then unlock the supply cupboard on the ground floor. Then, once he checked that he had all the necessary equipment, he would re-lock the front door and begin his rounds.

He'd been cleaning this building for several years, and although he enjoyed his job, it was always the 3rd floor that was the 'thorn in the side' of his working week.

... the 3rd floor. He always hated the 3rd floor; the sign said, 'Sales and Marketing.' But they were more like a chimpanzee house at the zoo. He'd been listening to a podcast called 'The Infinite Monkey Cage'; it was a kind of tradition; the 3rd floor looked like there'd been an infinite number of monkeys in there. It was 'In Our Time' for the lobby and 'Woman's Hour' for the ladies toilets.

Sometimes, he thought he should do the 3rd floor first, but he couldn't face it. Unfortunately, by the time he got to that floor after he'd worked his way through the whole building, he was tired and sweaty and not in a great mood. But he couldn't face doing the 3rd floor first. It was just too daunting, considering the condition in which they had left the place. He wouldn't let them work in a chicken shed, let alone a state-of-the-art office.

Perhaps he'd forgotten to secure it, and the wind blew, banging the door? Or maybe the mobile security team checked on all the properties across the estate. This was the first time that he actually began to feel a little nervous. It was 3:00 AM, and he was in the middle of a large industrial park. And he was very alone apart from possibly a few cleaners in other buildings and the odd mobile security patrol.

He made his way across the 3rd floor until he could see out of the windows overlooking the front of the building. What he saw puzzled him; it looked like a helicopter was sitting in the middle of the car park, but that made no sense. Nobody comes to work at 3:00 AM in a helicopter; nobody comes to work here in a helicopter at all. The shape wasn't quite right; there were no rotors on the top, but otherwise, it looked about a helicopter's shape and size.

Well, if it were the security team or a VIP making an unexpected visit, he'd better introduce himself. Then they'd actually know he turned up and did his job, even if there was nobody there to check up on him.

As he walked towards the main corridor leading to the stairs and the lifts, the lights all went out. Obviously, the lifts would not be an option, so he had to descend the stairs. It was an interesting coincidence that there was this helicopter in the car park, then the front door banging, and now the lights had gone out, and he was beginning to get a bit suspicious. Cautiously descending the fire exit stairs, he approached the entrance lobby.

Even the emergency lighting wasn't working correctly; it was flickering and intermittent, giving off very little light. However, there was some light from the street outside, which illuminated at least some of the lobby. As he approached, he saw a silhouette examining the glass door.

It was also clear to him that the door wasn't banging in the wind; it had slammed after being forced open. The aluminium frame was bent, the glass had broken, shattering into an intricate mosaic, and it was clear that someone had forced the door open with considerable strength.

The silhouetted figure was visible against the lights from the street, and so he approached it cautiously from behind.

There was something not quite right about the visitor's appearance. Perhaps they wore a face mask or a hood or hat, but the head looked the wrong shape. The Cleaner reached down towards his belt and grabbed his small torch. He always carried a range of tools; there was no point having to walk all the way back down the stairs to get something. He often carried out minor repairs in the building. On the one hand, he had his glass cleaner spray and, in the other hand, a small torch. Just as he got close to the silhouette, his foot must have scraped on the marble floor; he made a noise that sounded so loud in the silent building. The silhouette turned around, and as it did so, the Cleaner shone his torch straight in its face. The sight that greeted him took his breath away; it looked like 'Anubis', the Egyptian God.

Chapter 2 – 'Henry' Uses His Head.

It must be some plastic mask to hide their identity. The Cleaner squirted them in the face with the glass cleaning spray. The silhouette clutched at its face, moaning, howling and fell backwards. The Cleaner ran through the reception lobby and back up the stairs. He had decided the best thing he could do was barricade himself in one of the upper-floor rooms and ring the police.

As he raced up the stairs, his lungs were burning with the effort. Gasping for breath, he made it past the first and then onto the second floor; he decided this level would be the best option. This is where the senior managers were based; the offices were much more luxurious, but more importantly, they had good, solid doors, most of which were locked. The 'Sales and Marketing' on the 3rd floor was an 'open plan', but the second floor enjoyed considerable privacy.

Having reached the second-floor landing, he opened the small cleaners cupboard, which he rarely used, preferring to bring things from the main supply room on the ground level.

He looked about in the cupboard; there was almost valuable nothing in there, just an old 'Henry' taking it out; he looked around, sweat starting out on his skin as he heard the fire door leading into the stairwell from the ground floor slam, closely followed by the sound of ascending steps. Making his way back to the top of the stairs, he thought desperately about what to do. He'd used the glass cleaner spray, but that only worked if you could get close, getting close was not his preferred way of dealing with what were obviously burglars.

The steps were getting closer, the person, another 'Anubis', based on the silhouette, had reached the first floor and was just starting up the stairs to the mid-point landing, when the Cleaner had an idea, separating the vacuum cleaner's motor unit he swung it out on its flex in a wide ark, it dropped smoothly, like a pendulum, hitting the second 'Anubis' in the chest, there was a 'wooof' as the air was knocked out of the person and then the sound of him or her flying back across the landing and crashing into the fire door on the first floor, followed by the sound of the 'Henry' head hitting the tiles.

The first-floor doors were always locked, he never entered that floor, it was strictly 'Off-Limits' to anyone not authorised, it was where the real work was done. It had something to do with aircraft engines and other types of propulsion for satellites, there was that much on a board in the lobby for visitors to read.

Chapter 3 – What's The Plural Of Anubis?

He made his way through the second floor, searching desperately to find an office that was unlocked. The 3rd one he tried, the door opened, and slipping inside, he dragged the big heavy desk up against the door to wedge it shut. He made his way over towards the telephone, unfortunately, when he picked up the handset, there was no dialling tone. The phone was completely dead, and when he reached into his pocket and took out his mobile, he discovered that he had no signal.

He heard another sound. The fire door leading from the top of the fire exit stairs through to the second-floor landing had just banged shut. Someone or something had just entered the second-floor corridor, perhaps there'd been two of them on the stairs, and now they knew where he was. He went across to the glass partition and pulled aside the curtain just enough so that he could peek through. Again, although the illumination was very poor, he could just about make out a silhouette moving from door to door, testing each of the handles. What seemed bizarre to him was that the silhouette seemed to be struggling with the idea of door handles, as though it had never seen them before. But it was also clear this wasn't the same person that he had encountered in the reception lobby. That person had taken a face full of glass cleaner. He knew from accidentally spraying himself, that when it got into your eyes, it was really unpleasant. It didn't do any serious damage, but it was certainly very irritating. But this person didn't seem to be struggling, so perhaps it was a 3rd individual. How many 'Anubis's' or 'Anubii' were there? What was the plural of Anubis? The helicopter or whatever it was that was sitting in the car park wasn't very large, so it couldn't contain more than perhaps three or four people.

If he remembered his gangster movies, assuming these were thieves coming to steal something, then there would probably be a getaway driver still in the vehicle. So that meant there were only three people in the building, at least at a guess, so if he had managed to disable one of them in the reception lobby and another on the first-floor landing. That meant there was this one approaching him on the second floor of the building, and the 'driver', perhaps still in the vehicle.

Chapter 4 – It's Not A Mask.

He needed to disable this one, but how?

Picking up a desk lamp, he stretched the cable between the main desk and the coffee table, rapping it around the legs to secure it. Then moving over to the door, he moved the desk and ran back into the room. He crouched against the window and summoned up whatever courage he had left, everything up to that point had been *'fight or flight'*, this was the first time he'd had a chance to think about what he was doing. Taking out a screwdriver he tapped it loudly against the radiator, in the quiet building it might as well have been a church bell. He could hear someone trying the door handle and saw the silhouette shape enter the room, he'd not seen this before, but this one held what could have been a gun.

It immediately saw him cowering against the window and ran at him, snarling like an angry dog. It caught it's footing in the tight lamp cable and went face down, striking it's head hard on the oak floor, the gun object flying from its hand and under a large sofa. The 'burglar' was out cold, running forward the Cleaner dragged the body into the ensuite toilet and using a plastic tie, secured the wrists to the pipework under the sink.

Now was a chance to get a look at the burglars, maybe take a photo on his phone to show to the police when they arrived. Feeling around the head for the strap or something to release the mask, it quickly became clear to the increasingly scared Cleaner that it wasn't a mask and the furry gloves, weren't gloves at all. The hands or rather paws had fingers, but only three, the forth was very small and the thumb was in the wrong place, no wonder they had struggled with the door handles. They were about the same height as people, maybe a little shorter and tended to lean forwards as they walked.

Chapter 5 - Sorry I don't speak Dog.

As if the 3rd floor wasn't bad enough, now he had aliens to deal with. It occurred to him that a species could evolve from dogs, in the way humans had from primates, but to encounter one in the flesh was truly terrifying, as he sniffed the fur it even smelt canine.

Checking the straps that held the stunned 'Anubis' in place, he made his way across the office to the sofa and reached around underneath it to retrieve the 'gun'. Someone on the first floor would give their right arm to have a look at this. His hands didn't fit around the handle, it would probably take both hands to hold it, but now at least he was on a more even level. The questions were how to get help and where was the 'driver'? The second question answered itself as a bang of a slamming fire door warned him of someone approaching, the Cleaner crouched behind the sofa, aiming the gun at the door and hoping he had figured out the trigger mechanism.

There was a shape moving along the corridor, but as yet it was keeping clear of the doorway, a voice broke the silence and nearly the Cleaner's nerve. It was clearly artificial, although the 'Anubis's' hadn't used words, their grunts and growls had come from a living creature, this voice was synthetic, like someone using a computer program to translate.

"No shoot, please." Still no silhouette, maybe he could fire through the glass partition, but the Cleaner was curious. "I talk with you?" It was hard to discern if this was a question or a statement, there was no tome or inflection.

The Cleaner decided to try and reply, "ok."

There was a long pause, then "I come, please no shoot."

Again, the Cleaner limited himself to "ok."

A shape appeared in the doorway, the hands were empty, the Cleaner felt a little better, he didn't know what protection the sofa would offer if the creature fired. They stood facing each other, a kind of calm enclosed the room. The creature was whispering into something on their shoulder, it was then translating and speaking out loud. "We leave now; no hurt?" Again, it wasn't clear if this was a question or statement, were they telling him or asking his permission?

It had worked up until now, so why stop? "ok." But this time he tried to convey a positive tone.

The two beings stared at each other, the Cleaner was wondering if he should offer to play fetch or something, it was an almost primal urge, the creature appear so canine in its appearance and mannerisms.

The 'Anubis' driver, if that was what he was, the Cleaner suspected he was the leader of the 'pack', stared back, again the synthetic voice. "We leave, we fail, so now go." The soft brown puppy dog eyes made the Cleaner almost feel sorry for the mut.

The Cleaner felt a more eloquent dialog might be worth trying, the first floor would be desperate to know everything they could about the visitor.

Pointing to firstly the unconscious form in the ensuite and then to the 'leader' the Cleaner asked "Why have you come here?" He spoke slowly and clearly to allow the translation software to keep up.

The reply was sobering and puzzling. "We have studied you for many years, we all" pointing to the sky, "fear you."

They've visited Earth before, maybe to ancient Egypt, that's why their appearance was so similar to the Egyptian god. "Why fear us?"

The 'Leaders' reply had a mournful tone, "You are a very violent and warlike species, once you have space travel, we fear what you may do, we were sent to stop your development of a new propulsion system that will give you the stars." The translation system was improving as it learned new phrases and syntax.

The Cleaners thoughts turned to what usually happens to aliens in the movies, "I will help you collect your injured and then you must leave, soon others will come, there may be many questions and you will be trapped. Now you can warn your people to keep their distance from this world."

The Cleaner helped load their wounded back into the pseudo helicopter, they had made a mock up to appear as a helicopter at a distance but close up it was clearly something very different. There was an approaching sound of sirens, the security team had spotted the 'helicopter', along with the forced open door, and had rung the police.

The 'Leader of the Pack' turned and said, "thank you for sparing our lives you are a noble warrior." The Cleaner just coughed, nearly choking to hold back a laugh.

As the craft lifted off, he thought, shaking his head, 'Warrior'!? Turning, he made his way back towards the still unfinished 3rd floor. He needed to hide the 'gun' before the police arrived, they'd never look inside a 'Henry'.

Despite having visited Earth before, the 'Anubis's' hadn't learnt the lesson ... *You never mess with the cleaner!*

....

About the Author.

Member of Writers Anonymous. - *https://www.writersanonymous.co.uk/*

Member of The British Science Fiction Association. - *BSFA - Home*

I write a wide range of science fiction stories, both full novels and short stories. Covering subjects such as Humour; Post-apocalyptic; Space Adventures; Mysteries; Paranormal; Alien Invasion; Time Travel; & Robots.

Some are humorous, and others are more poignant and thought-provoking.

I'm a husband and a father, living in East Anglia, UK, and share my home with various animals, including dogs, cats, chickens, a duck and a goose.

When asked where I get my ideas from, I can only explain that my mind is like a septic tank; weird bits of, well, you know what, float to the surface from time to time and become the kernel of my stories.

As a middle-class, middle-aged, white bloke – If you need anything 'mansplaining', I'm here to help!

If you've enjoyed any of my stories, please leave me a review, either on Amazon or Goodreads.

https://www.amazon.com/author/brian terence

https://www.goodreads.com/author/show/52410012.Brian_Terence

Connect with me on :

https://uk.linkedin.com/in/brianterence42

BlueSky - @brianterence.bsky.social

Acknowledgements.

To Anka Troitsky for all her encouragement and advice. - *https://www.ankatroitsky.com/*

To Claire Cronshaw (Editor) for all her support - *https://cherryedits.com/*

No AI was used in the preparation of any of my manuscripts. All my work has been reviewed by my editing consultant - Claire @ Cherry Edits, prior to publication.